Néstor Ponce de León

The Book of Blood

Néstor Ponce de León

The Book of Blood

ISBN/EAN: 9783337389055

Printed in Europe, USA, Canada, Australia, Japan

Cover: Foto ©Andreas Hilbeck / pixelio.de

More available books at **www.hansebooks.com**

THE

BOOK OF BLOOD.

AN AUTHENTIC RECORD

OF

THE POLICY ADOPTED

BY

MODERN SPAIN

TO PUT AN END TO THE WAR FOR THE

INDEPENDENCE OF CUBA.

(OCTOBER 1868 TO NOVEMBER 10, 1873.)

NEW YORK:

N. PONCE de LEON, TRANSLATOR & PRINTER, 40 & 42 BROADWAY.

1873.

In consideration of the recent butcheries of Cubans, American citizens and English subjects, committed by the irresponsible Spanish Government of Cuba and the insult to the American flag in the seizure of the American steamship Virginius and subsequent shooting of her officers, crew and passengers, we deem it advantageous to place before the people of the United States and of England a rough sketch *almost exclusively compiled from Spanish sources*, of the carnival of blood that has taken place in Cuba during the governments of Generals Lersundi, Dulce, Caballero de Rodas, Ceballos, Pieltain and last but not least, Jovellar, those three last being representatives of the Spanish Republic.

We will exhibit first a catalogue of the persons murdered in cold blood by order of the Spanish Government of Cuba ; leaving out of consideration the killed on the battle field. We give with the name of each victim the source, in the most part spanish, from which we have taken the data.

We will also give a list of the names of those captured by the Spanish troops with arms in their hands since the 1st of March, 1869, taking them *always* from Spanish sources. We have selected the date because on the 12th of February a decree was issued and published in all the papers in Cuba, to shoot all the insurgents captured with arms in their hands. In this list we only include the names of those whose execution has not been noticed in the newspapers, and of whom no mention has ever been made ; but knowing as we do the law and the savage character of the rulers in Cuba, it is easy to understand what their fate has been.

The third list comprehends those condemned to death in the *garrote* by a military commission sitting in Havana but not executed on account of being out of the reach of the spanish hangman.

It will be well to bear in mind also that we always read in the Spanish reports that "Such a column has scoured such and such a terrritory and killed so many insurgents." Habitually the killed are poor, harmless and defenceless peasants forced out of their houses and brutally murdered.

We adjoin also a note of those delivered by the Captain General to the military courts as guilty of treason. We do not know the exact fate of those unfortunates. It is known, however, that many of them have mysteriously disappeared, and their families are sure that they have found an obscure grave in the burial grounds of the Cabaña or el Principe.

We do not pretend to give a table of the crimes committed in Havana and elsewhere, such for example as those at the theatre of Villanueva, the coffee house of the Louvre, the butchery of Cohner, Greenwald and many ilke cases : or the transcendentally treacherous killing of Augusto Arango under a flag of truce. Neither shall we attempt to catalogue the murders committed by the brutal soldiery in the country, the indiscriminate slaughter of defenceless men, women and children, the rapes, the obscene mutilations and the cruelties of every kind perpetrated in our unhappy country by the scourges of America : those are personal crimes which we do not deem just to charge upon a whole people.

In another list shall be found the names of those condemned to hard labour in the chain gang of the penal colonies of Africa or Cuba, many of them men of high standing who, often old and infirm, have been unable to endure the hardships and brutalities of their overseers and have been brought to an untimely death.

In another we publish the names of the unfortunate men sent to Fernando Poo, a barren and unhealthy island in the coast of Africa, a large number of whom perished on account of the bad treatment received on their voyage thither : all those lists are very incomplete as the Spanish censor permits the publication in the papers of only some of the crimes perpetrated in Cuba by *Modern Spain.*

We have not considered necessary to present the catalogue of persons whose property has been confiscated. We may only say that it reaches already the number of *eleven thousand,* a thousand of whom are ladies whose only crime is to be natives of Cuba and possessed of large properties there.

It is sought by some persons in this country to show that the Cubans have exhibited the same ferocity as the Spaniards in their conduct of the war, and that they have been uniformly as sanguinary and merciless as their adversary, uniformly as regardless of humanity as even Valmaseda. The allegation is utterly unfounded and grossly unjust to the Cubans, as those who make or credit it might easily satisfy themselves. In the very outset of the Revolution a considerable number of officers and men fell into the hands of the patriots, in Bayamo and elsewhere in the Oriente. All were spared without exception, and every effort was made by the cuban chiefs to carry on the war in accord with the christian spirit of the age. Many of these captive officers having taken their parole not to escape, have broken that parole, and became the most ruthless and unsparing of all the spanish officers in the war. Some also pretending to simpathize with the Revolution, took service under it and were trusted. Those for the most part betrayed their trust, deserted on the first opportunity, and like those who had broken their paroles, became conspicuous for their ferocity.

Meanwhile in all parts of the island no Cuban taken prisoner of war was spared ; to a man they were shot on the spot as so many dogs. Nevertheless up to August, 1869, many Spanish prisoners of war were captured and not executed by the Cubans. It was then that General Quesada endeavoured to bring the enemy to an agreement on the subject and addressed General Lesca a note to that effect. This note was published in the New York papers.

The reply was a verbal brutal of characteristic assertion of the Spanish adherence to the policy of shooting all prisoners of war ; leaving the cubans no other alternative than the stern measure of retaliation, which for a time, with many exceptions, was adopted on the Cuban side.

In October, 1869, General Quesada after having brought the matter to the notice of the Cuban Congress ordered that certain prisoners of war who had voluntarily taken service in the Cuban army, in number of 67 should be executed, they having been detected in a conspiracy to revolt under circumstances of peculiar treachery, these men were accordingly executed ; in a report of the affair made by General Quesada in 1870, by some error, the number was swollen to 670 or 603 more than were actually executed. The act excited a good deal of hard criticism in this country from the Press, in Congress and even by the President of the United States and the execution of so many men is cited as conclusive evidence of a blood-thirsty spirit in the Cubans quite equal to that of the enemy. Those who have taken that view surely overlook that the men in question were shot not as prisoners of war for *that they have long ceased to be,* as they had taken service under the Republic and were detected in a conspiracy to desert to the enemy ; therefore even had the number of those men been 670, their execution would have been a justifiable act of war. *

As to the cause of this execution we prefer to give Spanish evidence, namely, on account of the transaction from the *Diario de la Mariana* of the 24th March of 1870, which we translate: " All the officers, sergeants and corporals who were in the hands of the enemy have been shot. In connection with many Cubans they had planned a counter-revolution and had conceited the delivery of all the rebel chieftains to General Puello. Two days before the one appointed by this gallant general to commence his march, he sent a messenger to captain Troyano with the news of his advance. The bearer of the news was arrested however and searched, the letter was found, and on the following day the messenger, our officers and the Cubans compromised in the counter-revolution were shot, thus sealing with their lives their devotion to their beloved mother country."

Thus it is plain what those men designed to do. What the laws of war adjudge as the punishment of officers convicted of such crimes, will be found in any writer of international law whatever his nationality may be.

We deem proper to append some documents and extracts of documents, and papers, almost all from Spanish origin, which explain very forcibly the kind of war made by the Spaniards in Cuba.

COUNT VALMASEDA'S PROCLAMATION.

Inhabitants of the country ! The re-enforcements of troops that I have been waiting for have arrived ; with them I shall give protection to the good, and punish promptly those that still remain in rebellion against the government of the metropolis.

You know that I have pardoned those that have fought us with arms; that your wives, mothers, and sisters have found me in the unexpected protection that you have refused them. You know, also, that many of those I have pardoned have turned against us again.

Before such ingratitude, such villany, it is not possible for me to be the man that I have been ; there is no longer a place for a falsified neutrality ; he that is not for me is against me, and that my soldiers may know how to distinguish, you hear the order they carry :

1st. Every man, from the age of fifteen years, upward, found away from

---

* Americans must not forget the execution in Mexico, in 1848, of the Batallion of San Patrick, &c., &c.

his habitation, (finca,) and does not prove a justified motive therefor, will be shot.

2d. Every habitation unoccupied will be burned by the troops.

3d. Every habitation from which does not float a white flag, as a signal that its occupants desire peace, will be reduced to ashes.

Women that are not living at their own homes, or at the house of their relatives, will collect in the town of Jiguani, or Bayamo, where maintenance will be provided. Those who do not present themselves will be conducted forcibly.

The foregoing determinations will commence to take effect on the 14th of the present month.

EL CONDE DE VALMASEDA.

BAYAMO, April 4, 1869.

In the interest of Christian civilization and common humanity, I hope that this document is a forgery. If it be indeed genuine, the President instructs me *in the most forcible manner,* TO PROTEST AGAINST SUCH MODE OF WARFARE.

MR. FISH to
MR. LOPEZ ROBERTS.

MAY 10, 1869.

" . . . protesting against THE INFAMOUS PROCLAMATION of General Count of Valmaseda."

MR. FISH to MR. HALE.

MAY 11, 1869.

" Measures of war are undoubtedly those adopted by General Count of Valmaseda ; but they are not of such a nature as to revolt the feelings of humanity. Let the proclamation issued by General Count of Valmaseda be studied without passion, let the antecedents be recorded, and it will be seen that said proclamation *does not even reach what is required* by the necessities of war in the most civilized nations."

Leading article of the *Diario de la Mariana*, Havana.

MAY 9, 1869.

Captain Generalship of the Island of Cuba, Staff. The drumhead court-martial, sitting at this place on this day, with the object of examining and judging into the process instituted against the civilian José Valdez Nodarse, for having uttered seditious words, has condemned him to six years hard labor in the chain gang ; and his Excellency in conformity with the opinion of the Auditor has been pleased to approve said sentence, but recognising, as the Auditor does too great lenity in the sentence, because it is not in accord with the regulations, codes and existing laws ; he has ordered that the President and members of the Military Court may be sent to a castle to suffer the penalty of two months' imprisonment in the same.

Published by order of his Ex.

"With cheeks reddened with shame and hearts dripping blood, we confess, in view of what is now happening that foreigners are right. Africa commences in the Pyrenees, not the Africa of the Marochians, but the Africa of the Kaffirs."

Estado Catalan, Barcelona, August 9, 1869.

More than three hundred spies and conspirators are shot monthly in this jurisdiction. Myself alone, with my band, have already disposed of nine, and I will never be weary of killing.

Letter of Domingo Graiño, Captain of Volunteers,
September 23, 1869.

We captured seventeen, thirteen of whom were shot outright ; on dying they shouted hurrah for Free Cuba, hurrah for Independence. A mulatto said hurrah for Céspedes. On the following day we killed a Cuban officer and another man. Among the thirteen that we shot the first day were found three sons and their father ; the father witnessed the execution of his sons without even changing color, and when his turn came he said he died for the independence of his country. On coming back we brought along with us three carts filled with women and children, the families of those we had shot ; and they asked us to shoot them, because they would rather die than live among Spaniards.

Letter of Jesus Rivacoba, officer of Volunteers, Encrucijada,
September 4th, 1869.

Not a single Cuban will remain in this Island, because we shoot all those we find on the fields, on the farms and in every hovel.

Letter from Pedro Fardon, officer of Volunteers to Rosendo Rivas,
September 22d, 1869,

We do not leave a creature alive where we pass, be it man or animal. If we find cows we kill them ; if horses, ditto ; if hogs, ditto ; men, women or children, ditto ; as to the houses, we burn them ; so every one receives his due—the men in balls, the animals in bayonet-thrusts. The Island will remain a desert.

Letter from the same Pedro Fardon to his father, Sept. 22, 1869.

THE MARTYRS OF LIBERTY IN CUBA.

POLITICAL PRISONERS

EXECUTED SINCE THE COMMENCEMENT OF THE WAR WITH CUBA.

1868.

December.				
8 Manzanillo.	Hilario Tamayo--First patriot publicly executed	1	D.	19 Dec.
16 Cabo Cruz.	Four prisoners	4	"	25 "
22 Vicana.	One spy*	1	"	31 "
23 Manzanillo.	Theodore Bertot and the overseer of the sugar plantation Benicia	2	"	30 "

1869.

January.				
2 Pto. Príncipe.	One scout	1	"	8 Jan.
18 Ti-Arriba.	Col. Manuel Abreu, Lieut. Col. Francisco Abreu, Major Bernardo Delgado, Capt. Francisco Delgado	4	"	19 "
26 Guantánamo.	N. Parra and Juan Ant. Anaya	2	"	8 Feb.
February.				
9 Manzanillo.	"Some rebel chiefs, and many insurgents of whose fate only the earth that receives them in her bosom after they are shot, can render an account."	15	"	30 Mch
14 Jagüey-Grande.	Four prisoners	4	V. de C.	10 Feb.
17 " "	Elias Guerra	1	D.	21 "
22 Cienfuegos.	A Mexican general	1	"	26 "
24 Las Jíquimas.	José Lémos	1	"	26 "
March.				
1 Sagua.	Juan Daniel Araoz	1	V. de C.	3 Mch.
1 to 6. Cuba.	Five rebel chiefs	5	"	9 "

43

4 Remedios.	Teófilo del Pino and Cirilo Torres	2	V. de C.	12 Mch
8 Caibarien.	Five rebel chiefs	5	"	18 "
9 Cienfuegos.	Juan B. Capote	1	"	12 "
9 Peralejo.	Two spies	2	D.	3 Apr.
10 Villaclara.	N. Moya	1	"	21 Mch.
15 Remedios.	Dr. Francisco Jimenez y Rafael Falero	2	"	19 "
19 Colon.	Pedro Hernandez	1	"	22 "
20 San Anton.	Antonio Cadiz	1	N. Y. P.	
20 Corralfalso.	Juan Leiva	1	N. Y. P.	
21 Habana.	José Cándido Romero and another	2	D.	22 "
21 Bemba.	Juan Valdes and Loreto Indu	2	N. Y. P.	
23 St. Domingo.	José Fernandez Elvira	1	D.	16 Apr.
24 Caibarien.	Gustavo Valverde and Cristobal Pardo	2	N. Y. P.	
26 Alacranes.	Three brothers Olivera	3	D.	3 Apr.
24 Sagua la Chica.	Seven plantation burners	7	"	31 Mch.
26 Nieves.	Nicolas Oliva	1	N. Y. P.	
26 Lagunillas.	Manuel Guerra (engineer)	1	N. Y. P.	
27 Cuba.	Cornelio Robert	1	D.	11 Apr.
28 Villaclara.	Generoso de la Vega	1	"	17 "
29 Arimao.	N. Nodal	1.	"	9 "
30 Cuba.	Felix Tejada and Aurelio Castillo	2	"	10 "
30 Claudio.	Manuel Fuentes	1	N. Y. P.	
— Bemba.	Bonifacio Samaniego, Juan Fernandez, N. Garcia and Toribio Peña, killed by the "chapelgorris"	4	N. Y. P.	
— Guantánamo.	Manuel Borges, Professor of the Institute of Santiago de Cuba, and eighteen more sent to Guantánamo to be tried and shot in their way by the volunteers	19	N. Y. P.	

April.

1 Cárdenas.	The engineer Gerónimo Valladáres and a negro man	2	N. Y. P.	
2 Caibarien.	Ant. de Jesus Gutierrez	1	N. Y. P.	
2 Cobre.	Luis Guerra*	1	D.	10 Apr.
4 Cuba.	Adolfo Rodriguez and Francisco Puente y Medina	2	N Y. P.	
4 Isabelita.	One chinaman	1	D.	10 "
6 Holguin.	Justo Aguilera	1	"	16 "

115

			115		
7 Holguin.	Some prisoners of high rank		5	D.	16 Apr.
7 Horno.	Two brothers Aguilera and three more	.	5	"	6 May.
9 Habana.	Francisco Leon and Agustin Medina	.	2	"	10 Apr.
10 Nuevitas.	Benjamin Perez	.	1	"	16 "
11 Guisa.	Five prisoners	.	5	"	6 May.
12 Cuba.	One carrier	.	1	"	18 Apr.
13 Santa Clara.	Manuel Acosta y Bencomo		1	"	17 "
13 Gibara.	One letter carrier	.	1	"	30 "
15 Jagüey.	Two men captured in Zapata		2	N. Y. P.	
19 Manacas.	N. Medrano	.	1	D.	19 May.
20 Bayamo.	" Some large groups of enemies shot from the 13th to the 20th by Col. Palacios."	.	25	"	6 "
20 Dos Palmas.	Antonio Santa Rufina	.	1	"	19 "
23 Las Minas.	Fourteen rebels	.	14	"	15 "
23 Sagua.	Francisco Lopez Ramos		1	"	29 Apr.
24 Cuba.	Delfin Aguilera	.	1	"	6 May
27 Cartagena.	Twelve rebels	.	12	"	8 "
29 Cuba.	José Nicolás, Fernando, Ambrosio and Vicente Anaya, Homobono Portuondo	.	5	"	6 "
— Cobre.	N. Batista, Natalio Sales, Vicente Fonseca, Rafael Ruiz and two more	.	6	N. Y. P.	
-- Sevilla.	Three peasants	.	3	N. Y. P.	
May					
1 Bejucal.	Rafael M. Márquez*	.	1	N. Y. P.	
2 Manzanillo.	Many spies shot	.	10	D.	15 May.
2 Manacas.	N. Medrano, Juan Lachaitegnan " and nine more	.	11	N. Y. P.	
4 Cuba.	José Ant. Rodriguez	.	1	D.	16 May.
14 Sn Gerónimo.	José M. de Quesada	.	1	"	25 May.
16 Manzanillo.	N. Ardila and José Biritan		2	N. Y. P.	
19 Manzanillo.	Manuel La Rosa and an idiot shot by Machin	.	2	N. Y. P.	
20 Camajuaní.	Juan José and Pedro de Leon		2	N. Y. P.	
22 Cienfuegos.	Manuel de J. Ramirez, Ramon Cabrera y Benito C. Figueroa	.	3	D.	25 May.
19 to 25 Nipe.	Some prisoners of the Perit		5	"	29 "
31 Cienfuegos.	José Rafael Leiva	.	1	"	6 June.
June.					
2 Jibaro.	Luis Palmero, Andrés Meneses, Isidro Aquino and three sons*		6	"	N. Y. P.

252

4 Banao.	N. Serrano and a negroman	2	N. Y. P.	
4 Santa Clara.	Vicente Machado .	1	D.	9 June.
6 Cabaigan.	Cárlos Lucena .	1	N. Y. P.	
7 Guantánamo.	One pirate of the Grapeshot	1	D.	15 June.
10 Cuba.	Juan de Dios Palma, Jacobo Negrer and José Dooray	3		23 "
12 Cartagena.	Cirilo Arbona and Manuel Espinosa .	2		19 "
12 Baitiquerí.	Pedro Valdes, José Peña and Gregorio Rodriguez .	3		27 "
13 Santa Clara.	José Antonio Godoy	1		19 "
13 Santa Cruz.	Cárlos Polhamus .	1	N. Y. P.	
14 Santa Clara.	Manuel Vasquez .	1	D.	19 June.
15 Las Cruces.	A rebel .	1	"	19 "
15 Cuba.	Ricardo Sirven .	1	"	24 "
15 Palmillas.	N. Lamadrid, another man who was in prison and Luis Garcia .	3	N. Y. P.	
15 Roque.	Rafael Hernandez, and Juan Acosta .	2	N. Y. P.	
16 Macurijes.	"Five who had been pardoned."	5	N. Y. P.	
17 "	Diego Tavio, Manuel Tavio, and N. Espinosa .	3	N. Y. P.	
18 Colon.	Two spies .	2	D.	22 June.
18 Cuba.	Cárlos Speakman .	1	"	24 "
20 Santa Clara.	Cándido Roche ,	1	"	23 "
20 Cienfuegos.	Ant. de Armas y Castillo	1	"	24 "
21 Cuba.	Cárlos Quiñones, Martin Juztiz, Rafael Estevez, Juan C. Castillo and Alfredo Wyeth .	5	"	27 "
21 Santa Clara.	Felix Machado and Ramon Prieto .	2	"	30 "
22 Santa Clara.	Clemente Oliva .	1	"	27 "
23 Ramon.	N Rodriguez Colás .	1	"	7 July.
26 Baracoa.	José Bucelo and N. Calderin	2	"	14 "
28 Las Lajas.	Miguel Bonachea and Rafael Consnegra	2	"	2 "
— Arimao.	Ten stragglers shot .	10	"	14 "
— Camagüey.	Twenty-five rebels and their chiefs shot by Gonzales Boet .	27	"	2 Sept.
— Colon.	Francisco Puente, Eduardo Corrales, Manuel del Pino, Filomeno Facundo, N. Fundora, Miguel Hernandez, three brothers Valera, M.			

338

Almeida, L. Mendiondo, N. Samaniego, Urbano Rodri-guez, N. Castellanos, To-mas Garcia, Antonio Rob-inson, and two peasants, all shot by the "Chapel-gorris" of Guamutas, com-manded by the brothers Du-rante . 19 N. Y. P.

6 Bayamo. Juan and Manuel Fornaris, Luis Merconchini and his two sons Luis and Rodrigo, and nineteen more, Juan Gon-zalez, José Dumenigo, San-tiago Pujals, José Castella-nos, six of the Fajardo fam-ily, and fourteen neighbours of the hacienda La Punta, hanged head down by the Spaniards . 49 { Official report of General Marmol, June 25, 1869, published in La Revo-lucion, of the 1st of September.

July.				
1 Pto. Principe.	Agustin Socarras y Bonora	1	D	13 July.
2 Santa Clara.	Gonzalo Gonzalez and a negro man	2	"	7 "
2 Baracoa.	Five rebels	5	"	14 "
3 Cifuentes	Nine rebels	9	"	7 '
3 Manacas.	One spy	1	"	19 "
6 Cuba.	Notary N. Ferran and Manuel Estrada	2	N. Y. P.	
6 Puriales.	Torres father and son, and six more	8	D.	21 July,
6 Cabigan.	Ant. Arias, Natalio Machado, Angel Benitez and two sons	5	N. Y. P.	
7 Jiguani.	Dr. José A. Perez, Dr. Rafael Espin, José A. Collazo, Bruno Collazo, Salvador Benitez, Asencio Asencio, Joaquin Ros, Andres Villa-sana, Bartolo Montero, and their friends, Exuperancio Alvarez, Manuel Fresneda, Ant. Perez, Manuel Nate-ras, Manuel Benitez, a cook and six more who accompa-nied the nine first who were sent to Jiguani to be tried.			

<table>
<tr><td></td><td></td><td>439</td><td></td><td></td></tr>
</table>

	and assassinated and robbed in the march by Colonel Palacios (The Twenty-one of Jiguani)	21	N. Y. P.	
9 Puriales.	José and Pastor Pita and Casimiro Manresa	3	D.	14 July.
10 Scibabo.	Three rebels	3	"	13 "
10 Guá.	Twelve "	12	"	21 "
10 "	Pedro Cordero anp José Vila	2	"	21 "
10 Hongolosongo.	Ernesto Macarty	1	"	25 "
11 Sti. Spiritus.	One spy	1	"	19 "
12 Jibara.	Dr. Manuel de la Sera	1	"	30 "
16 Güira.	Francisco Torres	1	N. Y. P.	
20 Maguaraya.	Leandro Barreto	1	N. Y. P.	
23 Las Lajas.	Celestino de Cárdenas	1	D.	27 "
24 Ranchuelo.	Ceferino Perez	1	D.	27 "
29 Neiva.	Fernando Perdomo	1	D.	6 Aug.
30 Trinidad.	Patricio Parada and Francisco Fonseca	2	D.	3 Aug.
30 Cienfuegos.	Victorio Garcia, Felix Macias, Antonio Rodriguez del Rey, and seven more	11	N. Y. P.	
31 Caibarien.	Adolfo Ruiz	1	D.	4 Aug.
31 "	Antonio Perez, Anastasio Cortes and his brother and Francisco Priu	4	N. Y. P.	

August.

1 Camarones.	The chief Macias and sixteen rebels	17	D.	8 "
1 Tibisial.	Eight rebels "hunted"	8	D.	13 "
1 Vista Hermosa.	One prisoner	1	"	20 "
3 Guantánamo.	Teodoro Chayarran	1	"	1 Sept.
4 Mamon.	José Irene de Leon	1	"	14 Aug.
5 Potrerillo.	Jesus Ramos, Francisco Perez, Rafael Cabanuco	3	"	14 "
1 Güines.	Zacarias (a mulatto)	1	"	14 "
1 El Ramon.	The son of Rufino and another	2	"	27 "
8 Potreillo.	José Doroteo Perez, Antonio Herrera Alvarez and Silvestre Pedrosa	3	"	14 "
9 Cumanayagua.	Juan Castañon	1	"	14 "
11 Mataguá.	Francisco Fleites and Francisco Castro	2	"	17 "
11 Limones.	Bartolomé Martin and another	2	"	20 "
12 Yaguajay.	Two prisoners	2	"	17 "
12 Cumanayagua.	Two spies	2	"	24 "

<table>
<tr><td>552</td></tr>
</table>

552

15	Santa Clara.	Rafael y Miguel Sanchez	2	D.	24 Aug.
15	"	Patricio Nuñez and Agapito Lopez*	2	"	24 "
15	Caibarien.	Joaquin Espinosa y Perez	1	N. Y. P.	
18	Lajas.	Camilo Salgado	1	N. Y. P.	
19	Seibabo.	Two spies	2	N. Y. P.	
26	"	Juan B. and José Forte, his brother José and his slave Juan, Luis Gonzalez, Felipe Jorge, Salvador Rodriguez, the overseer of the plantation Adelaida and many others	13	"	"
20	Moron	Manuel Companiony	1	"	"
21	Trinidad.	José de la Rosa, Ramon Alvarez, Perfecto Quintana, Ladislao Lara and N. Arias.	5	"	"
21	Contreras.	Shot by Durante during the last three days, (some of them were distinguished persons and one was a planter seemingly very rich)	20	D.	24 "
23	Las Cruces.	Two prisoners	2	"	29 "
24	Candelaria.	Manuel Prieto	1	"	29 "
26	Jesus del Monte.	N. Cartas and brother	2	N. Y. P.	
27	Manicaragua.	José López	1	D.	14 Sept
29	Caibarien.	José Guevara, Joaquin Céspedes (90 years old) and one chinaman	2	N. Y. P.	
31	Cifuentes.	José Penton	1	D.	5 Sept
31	Niguas.	Twelve rebels of Callejas band	12	"	2 "
21	Baire.	Eighteen prisoners	18	"	10 "
September.					
1	Guá.	N. Santisteban, Rafael Torres, Gen. Pavon and some others	8	D.	8 Sept
1	Cidra.	Roman Sanchez (a chief) and another	2	"	15 "
2.	Sti. Spiritus.	Abelardo de Leon, Matias Cardoso, Modesto Jimenez, Francisco Montalvan and his clerk	5	N. Y. P.	
4	Esperanza.	Rafael Muñoz	1	D.	8 Sept
6	Hanábana.	Two guides	2	"	21 "
7	Sto. Domingo.	Julio Guzman, Fernando Divia, José Arredondo, Luis Jimenez and José Bosch	5	"	14 "

662

				662
7 Ranchuelo.	Manuel Portillo and three more	4	N. Y. P.	
7 Potrerillo.	A suttler	1	D.	17 Sept
10 Cidra.	Six rebels	6	"	15 "
14 Pto. Padre.	Manuel Trinidad Gonzales	1	"	28 "
16 Remedios.	Francisco Bacallao	1	N. Y. P.	
18 Ranchuelo.	Seven rebels	7	D.	21 Sept
20 Campechuela.	Three "	3	"	10 Oct.
20 Guanajay.	Nicolás Mendive	1	N. Y. P.	
20 Jutinicú.	Joaquin Mursuti and two nephews	3	"	"
20 Palmillas.	N. Valera, Perucho (a mulatto 80 years old) and ten more	12	"	"
21 Esperanza.	Fariñas and four more	5	D.	23 Sept
22 Recreo.	Nicolás S. Carballo	1	"	26 "
22 Cabaguan.	Three prisoners	3	"	1 Oct.
24 Caibarien.	Felipe Tarafa, Claudio Briñas, Julio Perez, and Dionisio Vazquez	4	N. Y. P.	
25 Remedios.	Two rebels	2	D.	28 Sept
25 Sta. Clara.	Máximo Grillo and a companion	2	"	30 "
26 Mayabon.	One rebel	1	"	30 "
26 Rio Hondo.	Eleuterio Cabrera, Antonio Vega, Eduardo, N., Silverio Cruz Escobar and Juan Valdes.	5	"	Nov.
October.				
8 Manzanillo.	Barrasa (the second of Marcano) Rafael Tornes Causo and Joaquin Palomino	3	"	21 Oct.
13 Santa Clara.	Tello Mendoza	1	"	14 "
19 Cartagena.	Desiderio Hernandez	1	"	23 "
19 El Roque.	Leoncio Guerra and two sons, Jacinto Oliveres, Cleto Daniel, Ignacio Camejo, two brothers Sardiñas and Desiderio del Aguila, killed by the Chapelgorris	9	N. Y. P.	
21 Santa Clara.	José Diaz Argüelles	1	D.	23 Oct.
21 Palo Picado.	Brigadiers Massó and Tamayo	2	D.	10 Nov.
November.				
2 Cienfuegos.	Antonio Luciano Sanz	1	D.	6 "
2 Guantánamo.	Arturo Casimajoux	1	D.	10 Nov.
2 Ciego de Avila.	Four prisoners	4	"	10 "

742

742

4 Trinidad.	Bernardino Rojas	1	D.	10 Nov.
5 Caunao.	Serafin Valdes	1	"	14 "
5 Sti. Spiritus.	Mateo Luis Perez	1	"	19 "
11 Cruces.	Four prisoners	4	"	14 "
15 Rio Negro.	One letter carrier	1	"	21 "
17 Jibara.	Abelardo de Leon, Bartolomé Martinez, N. Lopez, N. Montalvin, Luis Perez	5	N. Y. P.	
19 Sagua.	Francisco Barros	1	D.	27 "
19 "	Twelve chiefs of a negro plot	12	"	27 "
20 Dos Hermanas.	N. Real	1	D.	5 Dec.
20 Sti. Spiritus.	J. M. Madrigal	1	N. Y. P.	
21 Sti. Spiritus.	Enrique Ohlmeyer and Manuel Carbajal	2	D.	12 Dec.
21 Maguey.	One rebel	1	"	3 "
24 Tibisial.	Domingo Serrano, N. Olivera	2	D.	17 "
25 El Cristo.	Three rebels	3	"	7 "
25 Santa Clara.	José Prados	1	"	29 Nov
26 Holguin.	Carlos Tellez, Salvador Rivera, Francisco Valdes and N. Acosta	4	"	14 y 15 Dec.
27 Caunao.	Two prisoners	2	"	30 Nov
— Manzanillo.	Gregorio Santisteban Sr., Gregorio Santisteban, Jr., Juan Sanchez Izaguirre, Ramon Salazar, Antonio Roblejo José de Jesus Rosabal, Luis Betancourt, José V. Castellanos, Agustin Ramirez	9	N. Y. P.	
— C. de Zapata.	One spy	1	D.	2 Dec.
— Cuba.	Twenty five rebels shot by Gonzales Boet during his excursion,	25	"	14 "

December.

2 Guanabo.	N. Gonzalez	1	D.	7 Dec.
2 Santa Rita.	One rebel	1	"	7 "
3 Holguin.	Three salt-makers	3	"	15 "
10 Near Cienfuegos.	Carlos Consuegra	1	N. Y. P.	
14 San Luis.	Eustaquio Arencibia, Jacobo Montano, José R. Mendoza, Rafael Rivera, Domingo Aguiar, Juan Campos, Ciriaco Alvarez, Crispin Alvarez, Feliciano Campos, Gumersindo Galá	10	D.	19 Dec.
14 El Purial.	Ramon de Leon*	1	"	6 Jan.

837

15 Banao.	One prisoner	.	1	D.	6 Jan.
17 Ceiba.	One "	.	1	"	28 "
17 Cabagan.	Two who attempted to fly		2	"	28 "
18 Niguas.	One incendiary	.	1	"	22 "
20 Sagua.	Miguel Acosta y Epinosa		1	"	25 "
20 Niguas.	Nicolas Muñoz	.	1	N. Y. P.	
21 Macagua.	Dionisio Borges	.	1	" "	"
23 Arimao.	Three incendiaries	.	3	D.	26 Dec.
23 Cienfuegos.	Pablo Arvelo	.	1	"	26 "
24 Matanzas.	Eleuterio Lamar y Valera		1	"	25 "
25 Manacas.	Justo Pablo Meneses	.	1	"	6 Jan.
27 Santa Clara.	Two prisoners	.	2	"	1 "
28 Limones.	Two incendiaries	.	2	"	30 Dec.
28 Cabagan.	Ceferino Rodriguez	.	1	"	1 Jan.
28 Habana.	José R. Crespillo and Valdes Rubio	.	2	D.	28 Dec.
29 Cienfuegos.	Antonio Moreira	.	1	"	1 "
30 Pinar del Rio.	One incendiary and Telesforo Peña	.	2	"	6 "
30 Matanzas.	Pedro Rivera	.	1	N. Y. P.	
31 Villaclara.	Victor Carrazana	.	1	D.	4 Jan.
31 La Niña.	Two rebels	.	2	"	11 "
31 Las Tunas.	Mrs. Mercedes Varona and two prisoners	.	3	"	14 "

1870.

January.

1 Remedios.	One prisoner	.	1	D.	4 Jan.
1 Holguin.	José Guerra Almaguer and Captain Manzanedo	.	2	"	14 "
1 Sn. Isidoro.	One spy	.	1	"	31 "
1 Arroyo Hondo.	One traitor	.	1	"	31 "
2 " "	A negro rebel	.	1	"	8 Feb
5 Piñon.	Six rebels*	.	6	"	14 Jan.
6 Pinar del Rio.	Felipe Hernandez	.	1	"	6 "
6 Casilda.	One who carried bananas	.	1	"	11 "
7 Pto. Principe.	Ramon Sanchez	.	1	"	23 "
7 Palmarejo.	One prisoner	.	1		27 "
8 Sti. Spiritus.	Antonio Abad Bello	.	1	"	18 "
8 Güinia.	Three rebels	.	3	"	19 "
10 Sti. Spiritus.	Pedro Sanchez y Eligio Jimenez	.	2	"	22 "
11 Trinidad.	Pablo Lugones	.	1	"	14 "
12 "	Rafael Rodriguez Moya	.	1	"	14 "

892

11

			892		
12 Limones.	One prisoner	.	1	D.	27 Jan.
13 Arroyo Blanco.	Two spies	.	1	"	18 "
16 Trinidad.	Doctor N. Morado, Ricardo and Ramon M. Gras	.	3	"	19 "
17 Mamanayagua.	Five spies	.	5	"	8 Feb.
18 Cambute.	Thirteen prisoners	.	13	"	26 Jan.
19 Sagua.	One who uttered seditious words	.	1	"	21 "
21 Contramaestre.	Jesus Reyes, Santiago Duyende, an American colonel and four more	.	7	"	1 Feb.
24 Pto. Principe.	Miguel Esquivel	.	1	"	29 Jan.
24 Cubitas.	Sotero Napoles and another	.	2	"	12 Feb.
25 Ciego de Avila.	A Lieutenant	.	1	"	15 "
25 El Cedro.	Two prisoners*	.	2	"	15 "
26 Cuba.	General Francisco Marcano	.	1	"	2 "
28 Camagüey.	Sixteen captured by Goyeneche	.	16	"	6 " 6 "
31 Habana.	Two who uttered seditions words	.	2	"	1 "
31 Cuba.	Tomas Tamayo	.	1	N. Y. P.	
— "	Manuel Ros y Matias Hidalgo		2	N. Y. P.	
— Holguin.	Captain Miguel Rodriguez		1	N. Y. P.	
— Sti. Spiritus.	Luisa Fernandez y Gutierrez, a lady of 26 years of age condemned to death for the crime of concealing in her room a rebel—if executed, her execution, as many others, has not been published.	.	V. de C.		16 Jan.

February.

1 Pto. Principe.	Domingo Barreto	.	1	D.	8 Feb.
1 Trinidad.	Andres Matamoros	.	1	"	8 "
1 Cuba.	Lieutenant N. Ochoa	.	1	N. Y. P.	
1 Pto. Principe.	An artillery soldier	.	1	D.	8 Feb.
1 "	Francisco Silveira and three more	.	4	"	8 "
6 Polo Viejo.	A rebel prisoner	.	1	"	11 "
6 Guadalupe.	Four "	.	1	"	12 "
6 Arroyo Blanco.	Two "	.	2	"	12 "
6 Moron.	Three "	.	3	"	12 "
6 Magua.	N. Zerquera	.	1	"	14 "
7 Habana.	Felipe Valdes	.	1	N. Y. P.	
10 Charco Azul.	A post commissioner	.	1	D.	13 Feb.

974

974

3 to 10 Habana.	Thirteen (general order of Caballero de Rodas).	13	World	12 Feb.
14 Holguin.	Carlos Abreu, Eduardo Gazois, Francisco O'Ryan and Gregorio Caballero	4	D.	19 "
15 Sagua.	Manuel Sanchez and Joaquin Morales	2	"	19 "
15 Calabazar.	Juan Torrente	1	"	19 "
16 Yaguajay.	Five rebel prisoners	5	"	22 "
17 La Parras.	One " "	1	"	22 "
17 Bagá.	Two " "	2	"	22 "
17 Pto. Principe.	One " "	1	"	22 "
18 Santa Clara.	Six* " "	6	"	22 "
18 Holguin.	Manuel Oliva and two of the Goicouria expedition	3	"	2 Mch.
19 Pto. Principe.	Manuel Betancourt and N. Gonzales	2	"	2 "
19 Habana.	Jose Estevez	1	"	20 Feb.
20 Ceiba.	One prisoner	1	"	24 "
20 Santa Cruz.	Two "	2	"	8 Mch.
21 Cienfuegos.	Francisco Figueroa	1	"	24 Feb.
23 Holguin.	Four prisoners of the Goicouria expedition	4	"	3 Mch.
25 Cienfuegos.	Simon Calderon	1	"	1 "
25 Cascorro.	Miguel Fernandez	1	"	15 "
28 Juan Gines.	A prisoner	1	"	4 "
— Cobre.	Manuel Camacho, Belisario Caballero, José M. Bravo, Ventura Bravo, Juan Francisco Portuondo, Desiderio Echeverria, Juan Francisco del Pozo, Magin Robert, Ramon Garriga, Andres Puente, Joaquin Santisteban, Diego Vinagre, Melchor Catasus, Ventura Cruz, Baldomero Cosme, Diego Palacios and two more	18	"	25 Feb.

March.

1 Pozo Blanco.	One rebel	1	"	8 Mch.
3 Rubí.	Five rebels	5	"	8 "
4 Palmarejo.	Andres Sanchez	1	"	15 "
5 Palmarejo.	Two rebels chiefs	2	"	6 "
5 Pto. Principe.	Francisco Aldana y Suarez	1	"	15 "
5 L. del Infierno.	Five rebels	5	"	10 "
6 Polo Viejo.	One	1	"	12 "

1060

		1060		
1 to 8 Güines.	Thirty-eight of Arredondo's band	38	D.	13 Mch.
8 Sta. Ana.	Two rebels	2	"	17 "
1 to 8 Holguin.	More than fifty rebels captured and shot	51	"	12 "
14 Habana.	Julio C. Betancourt, Viscount Santa Cruz	1	"	15 "
14 Manicaragua.	N. Ballogina and two more	3	"	17 "
15 La Ceiba.	Merced Moya and Felix José Uiloa	2	"	18 "
" Güines.	Luis Arredondo and Rafael Cueto	2	"	18 "
" Pto. Principe.	Manuel Artola	1	"	23 "
15 Cobre.	Carlos Dubose	1	"	27 "
15 Cauto Abajo.	Sixteen conspirators	16	"	31 "
16 Güines.	Six more of Arredondo's band	6	"	17 "
17 Ciego Montero.	One rebel*	1	"	24 "
" Gibara.	Three rebels	3	"	30 "
17 Yareyal.	Joaquin Leiva and another	2	"	2 Apr.
20 Arroyo Blanco.	José M. Ecija and José M. Malló	2	"	5 "
" Moron.	N. Alpizar	1	"	24 Mar.
" Guanajayabo.	One incendiary	1	"	" "
21 Los Cocos.	N. Annio	1	"	" "
22 Sabana Grande.	José de la Vega Betancourt	1	"	29 "
23 Mayajigua.	Two rebels	2	"	1 Apr.
24 Matanzas.	Casimiro, Francisco and Juan Rivero, Antonio Cruz	4	"	26 Mar.
24 Cuba.	José Candelario Alayo	1	"	30 "
" Zapata.	Four rebels	4	N. Y. P.	
27 Pto. Principe.	Two repentant rebels	2	D.	2 Apr.
" Bayamo.	Ten conspirators	10	"	5 "
28 Cuba.	Agustin Lara, Isidro Rodriguez and Pablo Aguilera	3	"	" "
29 Cárdenas.	Andres Perez	1	"	30 Mar.
31 Guanabacoa.	José Vaso y Araoz	1	"	1 Apr.
31 Cuba.	Perfecto Perez	1	..	5 "

April.

1 Habana.	Eduardo Nattes	1	"	2 "
2 Pozo Azul.	Three rebels	3	"	5 "
4 Pto. Principe.	José S. Marrero and Lorenzo Torres	2	"	16 "
5 Sevilla.	General Oscart and José M. Fornaris	2	"	15 "
6 Cienfuegos.	Andres Diaz Castellanos	1	"	9 "
8 Pto. Principe.	Two spies	2	"	" "
" Ciego de Avila.	Three "	3	".	10 "

1238

		1238		
" Yamaqueyc.	Captain N. Parrado	1	D.	21 Apr.
10 Pto. Príncipe.	The American Officer Blake and a negro	2	"	14 "
14 Uruguay.	Julian Cheri	1	"	26 "
17 Holguin.	Eight of Peralta's band	8	"	30 "
18 Magarabomba.	Four rebels	4	"	21 "
21 Pto Príncipe.	Fernando Varela and Francisco Lopez Cámara	2	"	26 "
26 "	The Perfect Pedro Betancourt	1	"	1 May.
" Cabaniguan.	The rebel chief Fonseca	1	"	3 "
28 Yaguas.	Five conspirators	5	"	29 Apr.
" Báez.	One spy	1	"	1 May.
" Pto. Príncipe.	José M. Ralleti	1	"	2 "
30 Cienfugos,	Rev. Francisco Esquembre, parson of the parish of Yaguaramas (accused of having blessed the Cuban flag)	1	"	2 "
" Tierra Quemad.	Quirino Hurtado and Antonio Becerra	2	N. Y. P.	
May.				
1 Agüica.	Four rebels*	4	D.	4 May.
1 La Ceiba.	Serapio	1	"	10 "
2 Santi Spíritus.	José M. Benegas, Florencio Cañizares, José Gonzalez y N. Bermia	4	"	6 "
2 Limonos.	Four prisoners	4	"	12 "
3 Sta. Cruz.	Francisco Martinez	1	"	6 "
3 Caunao.	Some members of the families Molina and Adan	6	"	8 "
3 Pto. Príncipe.	Luciano Pruna y N. Castaneda	2	"	10 "
3 Salto del Cieno.	One spy	1	"	1 Jun.
5 Habana.	Fernando Rodriguez	1	"	6 May.
5 Pto. Príncipe.	Gonzalo Varona y Rafael Morales	2	"	10 "
6 Gibara.	Two spies	2	"	11 "
7 Habaua.	DOMINGO GOICOURIA	1	"	8 "
7 Buena Vista.	Tomás de Leon and Atanasio Bravo	2	"	16 "
8 Pto. Príncipe.	José Aldana	1	"	15 "
14 Habana.	Gaspar and Diego Agüero	2	"	14 "
14 Caimanera.	Emilio Torres Muñoz	1	"	3 Jun.
14 Najaza.	One letter carrier	1	"	2 "
17 Trinidad.	Juan Moya	1	"	27 May.
17 Arroyo Blanco.	Ramon Rodriguez	1	"	31 "
18 Cauto.	José Ant.° Castillo y José J. Feria	2	"	24 Jun.

		1308		
19 Habana.	Ricardo Casanova	1	"	19 May.
19 Sagua.	Pedro Dominguez and Fraustino Peraza	2	"	28 "
19 Mayajigua.	Two rebels	2	"	27 "
20 Santa Clara.	Ramon Chongo	1	"	22 "
21 Guanal.	Pedro Roblejo	1	"	24 Jun.
22 Pto. Príncipe.	Tiburcio Guerrero, Juan Antonio Perez, Manuel Tellez, Juan Brito, Francisco Batista, Pedro Gutierrez and another	7	"	31 May.
22 Rollete.	Three rebels	3	"	12 Jun.
24 Trinidad.	One letter carrier of Bembeta	1	"	5 "
25 Sti Spiritus.	Antonio Ramirez	1	"	10 "
26 Jibacoa.	José Cartaya	1	"	1 "
26 Pto. Príncipe.	Oscar Céspedes	1	"	3 "
29 Sitio Hondo.	One of Jesus del Sol band	1	"	2 "
29 Punta Brava.	Justo y Pedro Aparicio, José Valdés p N. Benavides	4	"	9 "
30 Yareyal.	Two rebels	2	"	10 "
30 Moron.	Joaquin Palmero and four more	5	"	16 "
31 Maraguan.	Luis Rivero	1	"	3 "
— Las Tunas.	Diego Milanes	1	N. Y. P.	
— Nuevitas.	Junta of Cubans, captured and punished	5	D.	13 "

1 San Agustin.	One negro rebel	1	"	12 Jun.
2 Cárdenas.	José M. Perez	1	3	3 "
3 Cienfuegos.	Higinio Moreira y Espinosa	1	"	3 "
3 Pinalito.	Fourteen rebels	14	"	22 "
3 Mayarí.	Carlos M. Delgado and seven more	8	"	22 "
3 Pto Príncipe.	Luis Medal, Tomás Almeida, Isidro Gance	3	"	8 "
3 Manzanillo.	Eduardo Hurst	1	World	10 Jun.
3 Trinidad.	José Zerquera	1	D.	10 "
7 Mayarí.	Alejandro Cutiña, Julian de las Rosas and Luis Carballo	3	"	12 "
8 Holguin.	Francisco Galobarde	1	"	23 "
9 Sto. Domingo,	José de la Merced Leon	1	"	12 "
9 Bijarrú.	Some rebels	5	"	28 "
12 Pto. Príncipe.	José Guiteras and Miguel Peralta	2	"	21 "
12 Remedios.	Pedro del Portal.	1	"	23 "

1391

1391

14 Santi Spíritus.	José Ramon Sanchez, Agustin Chaviano	2	D.	22 June.
18 Manzanillo.	Javier Villanueva, Vicente Céspedes and some stragglers	7	"	24 "
19 Manaca.	One scout	1	"	29 "
20 Guamutas.	Agustin Hernandez	1	"	23 "
20 Bocachica.	Salustiano Estevez and Nicolas Mendoza, shot on their sleep	2	"	25 "
20 Santi Spíritus.	One rebel	1	"	25 "
20 Gibara.	Antonio, Juan and Julian Naranjo, Valentin Hernandez and two more	6	"	25 "
20 Quemado.	Roman Pinto and another	2	"	25 "
20 Santi Spíritus.	Nazario de Lara	1	"	28 "
21 Pto. Príncipe.	Agapito Gerez	1	"	28 "
22 " "	Genaro Hijuelo, Benito Carun, José M. Arredondo y Eustaquio Chavero	4	"	29 "
22 Tunas.	Manuel Ruz	1	"	29 "
24 Cienfuegos.	A near relative of Jesus del Sol	1	"	28 "
24 Itabo.	Two rebels	2	"	29 "
25 Seibabo.	Juan Bruno and brother	2	"	3 July.
26 Pto. Príncipe.	Fernando Varona, José Francisco Fernandez and Gabriel Ballagas	3	"	5 "
27 Yaguas.	Tomás Almeida and three more	4	"	8 "
28 Habana.	Francisco Gonzales Junco	1	"	29 June.
28 Arroyo Blanco.	Miguel Garcia, José M. Perez and Juan Pazos	3	"	5 July.
28 Soledad.	Mongo Orduño	1	"	19 "
30 Pto. Príncipe.	Juan Caballero y Aguilera	1	"	5 "

July.

1 Santi Spíritus.	Antonio Lopez and Antonio Sirí	2	"	3 July.
1 Pto. Príncipe.	Hilario Perez and Francisco Medina	2	"	12 "
1 Holguin.	Manuel Mestre, Eulogio de la Calle, José A. Collazo, Isidro Portillo, Adolfo Leite Vidal, José Meana, and Agustin Batista	7	"	17 "

1449

1449

2 Cabaniguan.	Man Ramon Estrada, Luis Vega and six more	8	D.	20 July.
3 Giaya.	Three rebels	3	"	13 "
3 California.	" "	3	"	13 ".
5 Cienfuegos.	José Castilla and Juan Garcia	2	"	9 "
5 Pto. Príncipe.	Martin Lara	1	"	14 "
5 Malagueta.	Thirty-two letter carriers, spies and collectors of vegttables	32	"	17 "
6 Trilladeritas.	The rebel chief Hernandez	1	"	12 "
6 Calderon.	Cleto Torres, Miguel de los Santos Santisteban, Miguel Santisteban and Ramon Reyes*	4	"	17 "
7 Guabaciano.	José Salina and Manuel de la Sera	2	"	10 "
7 Sipiabo.	One rebel	1	"	15 "
7 Guabani.	One spy	1	"	28 "
7 San Luis.	Ignacio Santa Cruz Pacheco	1	N. Y. P.	
8 Guabaciano.	Two rebels	2	"	28 "
9 Manzanillo.	" "	2	"	17 "
9 Baire.	Many rebels	10	"	17 "
10 Trinidad.	Francisco Mendieta	1	D	12 July.
10 Vista Hermosa.	Rebel chief Francisco Molina and surgeon Rufino Napoles	2	"	17 "
10 Vista Hermosa.	Some stragglers shot	5	"	17 "
10 Candelas.	Manuel Rodriguez, Modesto Duche, Eusebio N.	3	"	17 "
11 C. de Zapata.	Two rebels	2	"	22 "
11 Sabanilla.	One carrier of provisions	1	"	28 "
14 Cumajuaní.	One rebel	1	"	22 "
16 Aguacate.	One carrier of bananas	1	"	20 "
16 Trinidad.	Two rebels	2	"	22 "
18 Laguna Grande.	Pablo Oxamendi, José de la Cruz Melendez, Ignacio Crespo, Juan J. Palomo, José Figueredo, Pablo Quiñones, Cárlos Perez Cisneros, Porfirio Garcia, Jesus Sanchez, Ignacio Forcade	10	"	4 Aug.
20 Bayamo.	Sergeant N. Moya	1	"	27 July.
20 Caunao.	Chucho Valdes	1	"	8 "
23 El Pesquero.	Nicanor, Luis, Jesus, Bernardo, Isaias y Fulgencio Reinaldo, Manuel Fuentes	7		28 "

1559

			1559		
24 Bayamo.	Dionisio Almena	.	1	D.	4 Aug.
26 Guajabani.	One rebel	.	1	"	30 July.
26 Narciso.	Two "		2		30 "
27 Mandinga.	One who carried provisions		1	"	4 Aug.
31 Bayamo.	Ant. Aguilera, and his son		10	"	10 "
August.					
3 Maguey.	Three surprised	.	3	"	12 "
8 Holguin.	Pedro Arias	.	1	"	13 "
8 Sti. Spíritus.	Hermenegildo Gonzalez		1	"	16 "
8 Mayajigua.	Manuel Conguegra, and Juan Valdes	.	2	"	20 "
14 Pto. Príncipe.	Julian J Pozo, and C. Moré		2	"	30 "
16 Sti. Spíritus.	Two rebels	.	2	"	18 "
16 Charco Redondo.	Five "	.	5	"	24 "
16 Holguin.	José Leite Vidal	.	1	"	24 "
17 Cuba.	Generals Pedro Figueredo, Rodrigo, and Ignacio Tamayo	.	3	"	24 "
17 Bayamo.	Brig. Angél Figueredo, Col. Manuel Fernandez	.	2	"	24 "
17 Pinos Blancos.	One rebel	.	1	"	25 "
20 St. Luis.	Juan Cortes (78 years) .		1	N. Y. P.	
20 Remedios.	Juan B. and Pedro Ferrer del Rio	.	1	"	31 Aug.
31 Cinco Villas.	Eight captured in different excursions	.	8	"	3 Sept.
31 Sti. Spíritus.	José and Francisco Ochavian, Francisco Caballero, Rafael Perez, and three armed rebels	.	7	"	3 "
31 Holguin.	Delfin Pavon, and seven more		8	"	14 "
— Banao.	Com. Gregorio Mola		1	N. Y. P.	
September.					
1 Santa Clara.	Felipe Acosta, and three more.		4	D.	7 "
1 Colon.	The spy N. Ruiz	.	1	"	7 "
2 Holguin.	N. Gonzales	.	1	"	1 Oct.
4 Gibara.	Marcelino N.		1	"	15 Sept.
4 Las Arenas.	Brig. Francisco Esteban Tamayo and Manuel Vega	.	2	"	7 Oct.
5 St. Domingo.	Merced Leon, José M. Castellon, Dionisio Diaz and Misterio Cardozo	.	4	"	10 Sept
5 Pto. Príncipe.	Vicente Velasco, Pedro Pelaez, Tomas Gomez, Federico - Cruz, Manuel Jimenez, Felipe Muñoz and Felix Pera	7	"	13 "

1631

			1681		
5 Trinidad.	Andres Llanes	.	1	D.	7 Sept
8 Sti. Spiritus.	Rafael Peralta	.	1	"	13 "
10 Pto. Principe.	Joaquin Espinosa	.	1	"	15 "
10 Sti. Spiritus.	Francisco Trueba	.	1	"	17 "
10 Pto. Principe.	N. Bonora	.	1	"	27 "
10 Pto. Principe.	Miss Pastora Lopez Marrero, a Cuban lady caught in arms was condemned by the military Court to be shot on the 10th of Sept. Her execution, if it ever took place, has not been published	.		"	14 "
11 Santa Clara.	José de los Santos Fleites		1	"	27 "
11 Santa Clara.	One rebel	.	1	"	13 "
12 Remedios.	Ant. C. Manso	.	1	N. Y. P.	
12 Fray Benito.	Eulogio y Leopoldo Sarmiento, Rafael Reyes, and Teófilo Lorca	.	4	D.	4 Oct.
14 Concepcion.	Two rebels	.	2	"	17 Sept
16 Baire.	Capt. Pedro Bertrandi	.	1	N. Y. P.	
19 Guinia.	Four rebels	.	4	D.	4 Oct.
22 Santa Clara.	Julian Perez del Hoyo	.	1	"	2 Sept
22 Jibacoa.	Cipriano Estrada, and Luz Medina	.	2	"	5 Oct.
24 Habana.	LUIS DE AYESTARIAN	.	1	"	25 Sept
24 Cayo Confites.	Three sailors of the Margaret and Jessie	.	3	"	7 Oct.
26 Santa Clara.	Joaquin Martinez	.	1	"	27 Sept
30 Holguinera.	Justo Aguilera, and another		2	"	18 Oct.
October.					
1 Cieguito.	Two rebels	.	2	"	4 Oct.
3 Sti. Spiritus.	One "	.	1	"	5 "
4 Gibara.	Three "	.	3	"	18 "
5 Cienfuegos.	Francisco Gutierrez Calvo		1	N. Y. P.	
10 Lechuzas.	One rebel	.	1	D.	25 "
12 Pto. Principe.	Manuel Torres Serrano, and Juan Martinez	.	2	"	26 "
13 Trinidad.	Dr. Vicente Rodriguez de la Barrera	.	1	"	18 "
14 Bejuco.	Clemente Cañizares, his brother and two more	.	4	D.	2
14 Matanzas.	Agripino Sanchez ; the Spanish papers call him a robber but he was condemned by the military court as a rebel.		1	N. Y. P.	
15 Sti. Spiritus.	Dámaso Leon.	,	1	D.	23 Oct.

1677

1677

16 Trinidad.	Andres Pimentel	.	1	D.	25 Oct.
18 Remedios.	Pref. Carlos Ruiz and Capt. Nicolas Loyola	.	2	"	4 Nov.
24 Camugiro.	Gen. Gabriel Fortun and fourteen more	.	12	"	4 "
29 Santa Clara.	Pantaleon Prieto	.	1	"	1 "
29 Yara.	Two rebels	.	2	"	9 "
31 Manajayabo.	Brijido and Julian Torres y Rodriguez	.	2	"	13 "
— Remedios.	Pedro Garcia and Agustin Ramos	.	2	"	25 Aug.
— Holguin.	Manuel Guerra Tamayo, Julian Patiño, Angel Aguilera and Carlos Druck	.	4	"	27 "
— Güines.	Francisco V. Garcia	.	1	N. Y. P.	

November.

2 San Pedro.	Three rebels	.	3	D.	19 Nov.
2 Paredones.	Alberto and Joaquin Moya		2	D.	8 "
2 Casiguas.	Two rebels	.	2	"	19 "
3 Manzanillo.	José Mendoza Lopez	.	1	N. Y. P.	
3 Colon.	Miguel Madruga	.	1	D.	11 Nov.
3 Paradones.	Inocencio Fonseca and Manuel Rodriguez	.	2	"	13 "
4 Tibicial.	Pref. Ramon Carbajal, Com. Armengol and another rebel		3	N. Y. P.	
4 Tempú.	Luis Varona and fifteen more		16	D.	18 "
6 Banao.	Miguel Silva	.	1	"	20 "
8 Holguin.	José Martinez and four more		5	N. Y. P.	
9 Maraguan.	Miguel Cepero and another		5	D.	15 Nov.
11 Trinidad.	Juan B. Pedrosa.	.	1	"	15 "
12 Pilatos.	Two rebels	.	2	D.	17 Nov.
12 Castaños.	One "	.	1	"	17 "
12 Canalito.	Pedro and Angel Reinaldo, Antonio Lopez and Rafael Fonseca	.	4	"	2 Dec.
12 Júcaro.	Raimundo Sanchez, Jesus Herrera and Ambrosio Zayas		3	"	20 "
13 Canasí.	Capt. José Lechuga	.	3	"	11 "
14 Yagruma.	One scout	.	1	"	22 "
15 Guaiva.	Two "	.	1	"	17 "
18 Jiguaní.	Quintilio Villareal	.	7	"	2 "
20 Sti. Spiritus.	Manuel Belen Perez	.	1	"	22 "
20 "	Manuel de Jesus Bahamonde		1	N. Y. P.	
20 Jagüey.	Federico Mola, José Gonzales, two letter carriers and another		5	D.	14 "
27 Cienfuegos.	German Barrios	.	1	"	1 "

1749

1749

27 Siguanca.	Capt. Alejo Cantero, Capt. Felix Yurubido and thirteen more	15	D	6 Dec.
28 Pto. Príncipe.	Cristóbal Mendóza	1	"	8 "
29 Hatico.	Com. Manuel Torres, Pref. Emilio Tellez, Subpref. Macias and some other officers	8	"	11 "

December.

1 Gibara.	One who smelt as a rebel	1	"	18 "
4 Las Tunas.	Three rebels	3	"	31 "
6 Momones.	Juan Meneses	1	"	10 "
7 Las Lomas.	N. Rodriguez	1	"	10 "
9 Los Cristales.	Emilio Moreno and another	2	"	14 "
11 Holguin.	Gen. José M. Aurrecoechea and his chief of staff Facundo Cable	2	"	22 "
17 Pto. Príncipe.	Lope Recio Agramonte	1	"	1 Jan.
17 California.	One armed rebel	1	"	15 "
19 Remedios.	Two rebels	2	"	23 Dec.
17 Pto. Príncipe.	Cap. Francisco Betancourt, Emilio Estrada, Carlos Torres, José Molina, Francisco Benavides, Manuel Montojo and Caballero, Javier B. Varona, Martin Loynaz y Miranda	8	"	1 Jan.
20 Holguin.	Manuel Zúñiga, Evaristo Torres, Francisco Llaurador, Miguel Peralta, Antonio Olivo, Antolin Varela, Santiago Miranda, Antonio del Toro	8	"	27 Dec.
21 Cienfuegos.	José Cayetano Santos	1	"	22 "
30 El Mamon.	One rebel	1	"	3 Jan.
15 to 30 Camagüey.	Eleven shot in different excursion	11	"	15 "
31 Trinidad.	A negro man.	1	"	4 "
31 "	Nicolas Fernandez	1	"	5 "
31 Guanaja.	Seven prisoners captured with the wife of President Céspedes	7	"	14 "
— Colon.	Antonio de Armas	1	"	15 "
— Canoa.	Segundo Bejerano and Antonio Avilos	2	"	20 "

1828

1871.

1828

January.

1 Santiago.	José Catasus, Tomas Stable and Mr. Marcetti	.	3	D.	7	June.
1 Vergel.	Two negro rebels	.	2	D.	4	Jan.
1 Cieguito.	Two rebels	.	2	"	10	"
1 Guisa.	Four rebels	.	4	"	4	"
7 Santiago.	Augusto A. Dominguez, Dr. Juan A. Corrales	.	2	"	14	"
9 Cienfuegos.	Mariano Guerra	.	1	"	13	"
9 Túnas.	Nineteen rebels	.	19	"	22	"
Camagüey.	Antonio Hernandez and two others	.	3	"	31	"
9 Holguin.	J. L. Ricardo and another	.	2	"	10	Feb.
15 Sti. Espíritu.	Two rebels	.	2	"	15	Jan.
23 Manzanillo.	R. Guardia y Céspedes	.	1	"	1	Feb.
23 Santiago.	Felipe L. Diaz, Juan Callejas and Severo Gonzales	.	1	"	1	"
24 Santiago.	L. J. Aguilera	.	1	"	8	"
24 Consolacion.	Two rebels	.	2	"	25	Jan.
25 Vuelta Abajo.	Felipe Rivero, P. Santana, F. Hernandez, N. M. Naranjo N. Nápoles, C. Planas, A. Mora, A. Estevez and F. Rodriguez		8	"	28	"
25 ti. Espíritu.	A mulatto	.	1	"	29	"
26 Cauto.	Pedro Mármol	.	1	"	8	Feb.
30 Esperanza.	Bernardino Valdes	.	1	"	2	"
February.						
1 Cienfuegos.	A. Rodriguez	. .	1	"	2	"
1 Trinidad.	M. de la C. Gomez, L. A. Jauregui	.	2	"	7	"
2 Cascorro.	Enrique Uranga	.	1	"	14	"
6 Margarita.	Eight rebels	.	8	"	1	Mch.
7 Las Lajas.	A negro who fled	.	1	"	1	"
7 San Jorge.	A rebel	.	1	"	1	"
7 S. Gerónimo.	Two rebels	.	2	"	10	"
8 Joiral.	Pedro Romero	.	1	"	17	"
8 Túnas.	F. Prieto, N. Milanés and Miguel Marti	.	3	"	23	"
13 Loreto.	A. Lopez Gutierrez	.	1	"	17	"
15 Ciego.	A rebel	.	1	"	1	"
16 Sti. Espíritu.	Plácido Peralta	,	1	"	24	Feb.
16 Jumento.	José Cerise	.	1	"	1	Mch.
17 Barajagüas.	A rebel	.	1	"	1	"
" Trinidad.	Leon Peña	.	1	"	1	"
" Moron.	A rebel	.	1	"	1	"

1918

			1918		
17 Sagua.	Brígido Ferrer	.	1	D	23 Feb.
19 Sti. Espíritu.	A postman	.	1	"	21 "
" Naranjo.	A postman	.	1	"	1 Mch.
23 Camagüey.	C. Sosa, E. Miranda Provost Sergeant Callejas	.	3	"	12 "
" Guaramena.	Seventeen rebels	.	17	D.	17 Mch.
26 Juan Sanchez.	Majors M. Perdomo and S. Milá, Capt. A. Paredes, Lieut. E. Rivero, J. B. Agramonte, J. Martinez, P. Ibarra, B. Leiva and F. Echemendia	.	10	"	12 "
" Casanova.	Nine shot	. .	9	"	19 "
28 San José.	A man	.	1	"	17 "

March.

1 Trinidad.	Miguel Gollo	.	1	D.	14 Mch
" Balume.	Camilo Carnesoltas	.	1	"	17 "
3 Villar.	A negro	.	1	"	30 "
6 Caunao.	M. Cervantes, José de Jesus del Sol, Rafael del Sol, M. Hernandez and F. Rodriguez.		5	"	15 "
8 Cienfuegos.	Carlos Cerise and Salomé Moya Hernandez	.	2	"	10 "
" Moron.	Fernando Estrada	.	2	"	10 "
9 Guayabal.	F. Fernandez, F. Martinez, José Valdivia, J. Compañon		4	"	11 "
" Mijial.	Fernando Perez	.	1	"	11 "
15 Entre Cedros.	Manuel P. Quintanilla, B. Marron, P. J. Tamayo and two other rebels	.	5	"	16 Apr.
" Pico Blanco.	G. Caridad, N. Rodriguez, J. Aguilar Montalvan	.	3	"	17 Mar.
" Trocha.	A rebel	.	1	"	" '
" Caunao.	A man shot	.	1	"	" "
" Punta.	Three rebels	.	3	"	" "
" Guillos.	A rebel	.	1	"	" "
16 Túnas.	Four rebels	.	4	"	30 "
" Casanova.	Eight rebels	.	8	D.	19 Mch.
17 Maya Larga.	Luis Lavielle	.	1	"	15 Apr.
" Vega Vieja.	Three rebels	.	3	"	17 Mar.
" Barajaguas.	Five rebels	.	5	"	18 "
18 Bartolomé.	Leon Lara	.	1	"	30 "
" Sti. Espíritu.	Pedro Martinez, Joaquin Guijarro	.	2	"	30 "
" S. Joaquin.	Six rebels	.	6	"	30 "
21 La Vega.	José Manuel Quesada (75 years old) for the *crime* of being				

2022

	uncle to General Quesada	1	D	11 Apr.
21 Jicotéa.	One rebel	1	"	" "
" Barrancas.	Five rebels	5	"	16 "
25 Cabreras.	M. Zaldivar and another	2	"	" "
27 Trinidad.	J. Marcano and Magdaleno Polanco	2	"	2 "
29 Nazareno.	Juan de Dios Cruz	1	"	16 "
April.				
1 Guanaja.	Two rebels	2	"	" "
" "	José R. Ponte, Gerónimo Rodriguez, P. Carmenati, F. Cabreras and a negro	5	"	" "
2 Cedro.	Five rebels	5	"	" "
4 Santi Spíritus.	Arcadio Garcia	1	"	8 Aug
6 Nicho.	Three rebels	3	"	16 Apr.
7 Montaño.	Four "	4	"	12 "
" Enceibas.	Three "	3	"	30 "
" Demajagua.	Five "	5	"	30 "
8 Guaney.	Roman Hernandez	1	"	" "
11 Samá.	Three rebels	3	"	" "
13 Listas.	Six "	6	"	16 "
22 Santiago.	Five "	5	"	25 "
" Meliton.	Lieut. B. Salinas, M. Sanchez and F. Cabrera, C. Martinez and R. Gonzales	5	"	27 "
24 Santiago.	Roque Trujillo	1	"	30 "
25 Guadacacoa.	One rebel	2	"	2 May
" Ciénega.	Captain Coronas	1	"	" "
26 Jobosí.	Miguel G. Gutierrez (member of Cuban Congress) and another			
25 Las Villas.	Five rebels	5	"	1 "
May.				
1 Las Lajas.	One rebel	1	D.	3 June.
2 La Vega.	Leon and another	1	"	14 May.
4 Guásimas.	Meliton Ramos and Joré Bitorla	2	"	9 "
3 Arroyo Blanco.	One rebel	1	"	4 "
5 Hondones.	J. M. Escancio	1	"	3 June.
9 Cascorro.	Two spies	2	"	9 "
" Babosa.	Juan Torres	1	"	25 May.
10 Salinas.	Carlos Peña and Camilo Velazquez	2	"	21 "
13 Nuevitas.	Enrique Flotas	1	"	" "
11 La Sagua.	Col. Pascual Beauvilliers, Capt. Antonio Bachiller, Lieuts. Pedro Lecerff and Ricardo			

2103

		2103		
	Piñeyro, N.Lopez, Pio Miliano, Mariano Silva, Pablo Sedeño and Miguel Hurtado .	9	D. '	21 May.
13 La Saqua.	General Manuel Boza Agramonte .	1	"	" "
14 Nuevitas.	Captain Carlos Varona .	1	"	" "
" Cobre.	Four of the Moya family .	4	"	" "
" Sn. Miguel.	Ramon Torres .	1	"	9 June.
15 Guaney.	Carlos Rivero .	1	"	21 May.
" Placetas.	Two incendiaries .	2	"	20 "
" Jiguaní.	Marcelo Ramirez, Juan Cañote, Fernando Guzman and four rebels .	7	"	25 "
16 Guananí.	One rebel .	1	"	9 June.
17 Holguin.	One spy .	1	"	16 "
20 Habana.	Juan Marquez Garcia	1	"	21 May.
" Santiago.	Fifteen rebels .	15	"	30 "
" Cobre.	Cárlos and José Botta, Cárlos Garay and N. Guardia	4	"	31 "
22 "	One rebel .	1	"	16 June.
25 Guáimaro.	Pedro Riso and seven rebels	7	"	9 "
27 Agirte.	Marcelino Fernandez .	1	"	16 "
30 San Luis.	Five rebels .	5	"	14 "

June.

2 Puerto Principe.	Peregrin Rodriguez .	1	"	7 "
" Cauto Abajo.	Two rebels .	2	"	1 July.
18 Perú.	Four " .	4	"	14 June.
6 Vertientes.	Two " .	2	"	" "
10 Vega.	Cárlos Piña and Camilo Velazquez .	2	"	16 "
11 Cascorro.	Two spies .	2	"	16 "
17 Esperanza.	One rebel .	1	"	1 July.
18 Remedios.	Col. Novell, Charles Westrup and six more .	8	"	30 "
23 Pirindingo.	P. Zancas and one negro	2	"	1 "
25 Las Tunas.	Six rebels .	6	"	4 "
29 "	Three rebels .	3	"	21 "
31 Jucaro.	Eduardo del Mármol .	1	"	27 "

July.

1 Chorrera.	Twelve rebels .	12	"	8 "
2 Ciego de Avila.	José Botellas, Pascual Osorio and Eduardo Toraya .	3	"	11 "
" Camajuaní.	Juan Rodriguez and another	2	"	4 Aug.

2216

2216

4	Ciego de Avila.	One rebel	.	1	D.	12 July.
"	Moron.	Two rebels	.	2	"	" "
6	Vapor Neptuno.	Juan Bautista Osorio	.	1	"	15 "
"	Puerto Principe.	General Federico Cabada		1	"	" "
7	Santa Ana.	Andres Tamayo	.	1	"	25 "
9	Aguadas.	Three rebels	.	3	"	16 "
11	Júcaro.	Manuel Rodriguez	.	1	"	18 "
12	Limones.	Two rebels	.	2	"	16 "
14	Sti. Spíritus.	Francisco Alvarez	.	1	"	25 "
15	"	General Leon Tamayo	.	1	"	16 "
16	Villaclara.	Two rebels	.	2	"	21 "
"	Hoyos.	Antonio Montejo and son		2	"	1 Aug.
19	Júcaro.	Brig. Gen. Guillermo Lorda and Col. Chucho Consuegra		2	"	20 July.
"	Pto. Príncipe.	Felipe Aug.º Baqué	.	1	"	25 "
22	Cinco Villas.	One rebel	.	1	"	1 Aug.
23	Ciego de Avila.	Four rebels	.	4	"	15 "
24	Trapiche.	One rebel	.	1	"	1 "
24	Camajuaní.	Ramon Castañeda, Cárlo Gomez and another man	.	3	"	8 "
25	Manatí.	One rebel	.	1	"	16 "
26	Rio Sevilla.	Two rebels	.	2	"	16 "
"	Cupeyes.	Five rebels	.	5	"	8 "
27	Cuero.	Basilio Fernandez	.	1	"	3 "
28	Guanabo.	One rebel.	.	1	"	30 July.
30	Moron.	Four rebels	.	4	"	8 Aug.

August.

4	Santiago.	Col. Miguel Figueredo and Cárlos Quesada	.	2	"	11 "
"	Manzanillo.	One rebel	.	1	"	" "
5	Moron.	Manuel Gonzales, Cap. Sev Ramos and three more	.	5	"	16 "
9	Trinidad.	Bernardino Maruri	.	1	"	15 "
10	Iguará.	One rebel	.	1	"	" "
"	Sti. Spíritus.	Manuel Fresneda	.	1	"	" "
12	Santiago.	Juan Castro, Nicolas Boudet and José Gonzales	.	3	"	19 "
14	Palmarejo.	Lorenzo Ortego	.	1	"	22 "
15	Gibaro.	One deserter	.	1	"	31 "
16	Holguin.	Four rebels	.	4	"	16 "
"	Palmasola.	One "	.	1	"	17 "
"	Sti. Spíritus.	One "	.	1	"	17 "
"	Las Cruces.	One "	.	1	"	31 "
17	Manzanillo.	Rafael Garcia	.	1	"	26 "
19	Moron.	Col. Fernando Callejas	.	1	"	25 "

2288

			2288		
22 San Joé.	Four men in hospital	.	4	D	29 Aug.
" Ciuco Villas.	The prefect of Higuerita		1	"	30 "
25 Habana.	Juan Clemente Zenea	.	1	"	26 "

September.

5 San Martin.	Dionisio Márquez	.	1	"	7 Sept.
6 Mayajigua.	Guillermo Fernandez	.	1	"	16 "
10 Cinco Villas.	One rebel	.	1	"	21 "
14 Villa Clara.	Two rebels	.	2	"	7 "
15 La Palma.	One rebel	.	1	"	23 "
16 Sta. Inés.	Manuel Gonzales	.	1	"	27 Oct.
18 Camajuaní.	One rebel	.	1	"	23 Sept.
20 Canoa.	Two rebels	.	2	"	1 Oct.
25 Rio Salado.	One rebel	.	1	"	17 "
27 Túnas.	Serapio Arteaga y Fran.° Castillo	.	2	"	17 "
" Manatí.	One rebel	.	1	"	17 "
30 Artemisa.	One "	.	1	"	17 "

October.

5 Holguin.	Antonio Garayalde	.	1	D.	15 Oct.
6 Sagua.	One rebel	.	1	"	10 "
" Ramirez.	One chinaman	.	1	"	" "
23 Las Túnas.	Tomas Perez Roman	.	1	"	14 Nov.
24 Dormitorio.	Pedro Duarte	.	1	"	" "
" Yamaqueyes.	A prisoner murdered by the Spanish corporal, A. Camacho	1	"	17 "
29 Mal Pais.	Col. Eugenio Odoardo, Augusto Odio and two negroes	4	"	14 "
" Nazareno.	One rebel	.	1	"	17 "

November.

3 Pino.	Ramon Gonzales	.	1	D.	1 Dec•
5 López.	Juan Varona	.	1	"	17 Nov·
7 Ciego.	One sutler	.	1	"	12 Dec·
8 Camaguey.	Majors Pedro C. Garcia and José del Cármen Rosabal	.	2	"	14 Nov.
" Trinidad.	One rebel	.	1	"	12 Dec.
9 Ciego.	One spy	.	1	"	17 Nov.
" Güiral.	One rebel	.	1	"	12 Dec.
10 Fajá.	Two "	.	2	"	14 "
" Palma Sorrino.	Four "	.	4	"	1 "
14 Camarones.	One "	.	1	"	23 Nov.
" San Mateo.	Col. Delgado	,	1	"	1 Dec.
15 Peña.	One rebel	:	1	"	12 "
16 Sabanalamar,	Colonel José Ramon Estrada		1	"	22 Nov

2337

			2337		
16 Jobosí.	Cârlos Rodriguez	.	1	D.	23 Nov.
17 Villa Clara.	Marcos Quesada	.	1	"	21 "
" Manteca.	A mulatto	.	1	"	1 Dec.
18 Caimito.	Two rebels	.	2	"	12 "
20 Palomita.	One rebel	.	1	"	" "
21 Asiento Viejo.	Eugenio Verdesia and another	2	"	1 "
" Loma Alta.	One sickman	.	1	'	14 "
" Santiago.	One negroman and another	2	"	16 "
·' Pedro Barba.	One rebel	.	1	"	" "
" St. Spíritus.	Three rebels	.	3	"	" "
21 Cachara.	Three provision carriers	3	"	" "
22 Tayabo.	One rebel	.	1	"	1 "
" Guaimaro.	N. Soler	.	1	"	" "
24 Caimito.	One rebel	.	1	"	14 "
26 Pozo Salado.	One rebel	.	1	"	12 "
27 Habana.	The Medical Students ALÓNSO ALVAREZ DE LA CAMPA, JOSE M. MEDINA Y SILVA, CARLOS AUGUSTO LATORRE, ELADIO GONZALES TOLEDO, PASCUAL RODRIGUEZ Y PEREZ, ANASTASIO BERMUDEZ, ANGEL LABORDE, CARLOS VERDUGO	8	"	28 Nov.
29 Guaicanamar.	Fran.° Agramonte, Eduardo Alvarez, Domingo Boada and Juan Basulto	.	4	"	14 Dec.

December.

3 Sant. Spíritus.	José Salvador and a chinaman	2	D.	6 Jan.
4 Santa Rosa.	Two rebels	.	2	"	16 Dec.
" Leonero.	Ramon Estrada	.	1	"	" "
17 Guaniminal.	One rebel	.	1	"	20 "
20 Camajuani.	One "	.	1	"	22 "
" Ciego de Avila.	The postman Isaac	.	1	"	29 "
" Llanadas.	Two rebels	.	2	"	30 "
20 Trinidad.	Two rebels.	.	2	"	31 '
" Sn. José.	Manuel Planas and two more	3	"	" "
" Chorrillo.	Two rebels	.	2	"	" "
" Negros.	One rebel	.	1	"	" "
" Prosperidad.	Two rebels	.	2	"	" "
25 Guáimaro.	Ramon Hernandez and four more	.	5	"	9 Jan.
27 Los Yareyes.	Two rebels	.	2	"	10 "
30 Guáimaro.	Antonio and Loreto Rivas and Salvador Oramas	.	3	"	6 "
31 Jimirú.	Luis Maria Jimenez and two more	.	3	"	4 "

			2403

1872.

2403

1	Sabanalamar.	A negro man	1	D.	18 Jan.
4	Purgatorio.	José Salvador and three more	4	"	" "
5	Sabanilla.	One rebel	1	"	11 "
"	Sant. Spiritus.	Col. Emilio Espinosa	1	"	13 "
"	La Deseada.	Three rebels	1	"	18 "
"	Chorrillo.	MiguelR ivero and our more	5	"	" "
"	Caimito.	Pedro Be lo	1	"	" "
6	Trinidad.	Three rebels.	3	"	14 "
8	Capiro.	Two rebels	2	"	18 "
12	Las Tunas.	Eduardo Saavedra	1	"	26 "
14	Sta Clara.	A negro man	1	"	28 "
15	Güinia.	A rebel	1	"	25 "
"	St. Spiritus.	Andrés Blanco, A. Figueredo, M. de los Rios, I. C. Orozco, M. Peraza, A. W. Seriol and five negroes	11	"	25 "
19	Guanales.	Cristóbal Pardo	1	"	31 "
21	El Corojo.	One rebel	1	"	28 "
22	Cauto.	A de la Hoz	1	"	16 Feb.
24	Sta Clara.	Manuel López	1	"	28 Jan.
25	Sierrezuela	Miguel Quesada	1	"	28 "
"	San Miguel.	One rebel	1	"	" "
"	Ciego de Avila.	Juan Luis Artosa	1	"	31 "
27	Los Güiros.	One rebel	1	"	" "
"	Moron.	Two rebels without arms	2	"	16 Feb.
28	Ciego de Avila.	Mateo Casanova	1	D.	8 "

1	Guayabal.	The sickmen in the hospital of Vicente García, T. Gonzales, A. Agüero, F. Rodriguez, I. Perez, R. Peña, A. Trujillo, M. Fonseca, P. Gonzalez, M. Roblejo, M. Prieto and Nicolas Roque	11	"	15 "
"	Manicaragua.	One rebel	1	"	16 "
3	La Palma.	Two rebels	2	"	1 Mch.
"	Rio Blanco.	Capt. Lorenzo Odoardo and eight soldiers	9	"	" "
6	Pto Príncipe.	Fran. Almanza and Miguel Ayala	2	"	17 Feb.
7	Guamurí.	Two sick rebels	2	"	28 "

2473

2473

13 Guayacabo.	Alejandro Perez and Vicente Sosa	2	D.	19 Feb.	
18 Ciego de Avila.	Manuel Menié	1	"	" "	
" "	A rebel	1	"	20 "	
14 Guayabal.	José Tomas, Luis Nápoles, Francisco Hernandez and another	4	"	28 "	
18 Cuba.	Two officers and a corporal	3	"	21 "	
21 Hato Viejo.	Three rebels	3	"	24 "	

March.

1 Guáimaro.	Cárlos Morgado and two prisoners	3	"	14 Mch.
11 Cascorro.	Pablo Navarro, Diego Mendez and three more	5	"	28 "
" Nazareno.	Seven prisoners shot	7	"	" "
13 Cacagual.	One chinaman	1	"	30 Apr.
15 Sevilla.	Pedro A. Ramos	1	"	30 Mch.
27 Trinidad.	Lico Peña	1	"	2 Apr.
30 Jagüey.	Cap. Ignacio Roberto	1	"	14 "
31 Las Túnas.	Eight rebels	8	"	13 Jun.

April.

11 Jiquí.	One spy	1	"	8 May
" Güiro.	A hospital with ten sick men	10	"	25 Jun.
12 Santiago.	Angel Alvarez	1	"	20 Apr.
16 El Jobo.	Two rebels	2	"	20 "
19 San Lorenzo.	Two "	2	"	8 May
23 Nuevitas.	Five rebels	5	"	28 Apr.
29 Dolores.	Colonel Varona, Majors Agüero and Junco, Capt. F. Quesada, Rómulo Riveron, A. Curico, F. I. Guevara and four more	11	"	12 May

May.

2 Guasimal.	One rebel	1	"	12 "
5 Dolores.	Prefect José Adam and brother	2	"	" "
9 Itabos.	Nine rebels	9	"	31 "
12 Jaguales.	Two rebels.	2	"	16 "
14 San Miguel.	Col. Jaime Moreno two sons and a negro	4	"	18 "
15 Güiros.	Juan Estrada	1	"	31 "
17 Salvial.	Nine rebels	9	"	18 "
19 San Cayetano.	Two captains, one prefect, the "Bayames" and another	5	"	31 "
26 Manao,	D. Perez and another ,	2	"	29 "

2585

2585

26 Cuba.	Luciano Rubicnes and eighteen more	.	19	D.	30 May.
30 Jagüeyes.	One rebel	.	1	"	11 Jun.
31 Moron.	Felix Torres	.	1	"	9 "
" Las Túnas.	Pablo Iriarte, Joaqnin Aldana, Jesus and Luis Osorio and thirteen other rebels	.	18	"	11 "
June.					
7 Mamcy.	Three rebels	.	3	"	18 "
14 Puerto Príncipe.	Probost Salvador Gonzales		1	"	26 "
15 "	General José Inclan, Major Tomás de Varona and one negro	.	3	"	18 "
17 Quijada.	Thirteen rebels	.	13	"	20 "
21 Las Yoguas.	Majors Francisco Drago and Antonio Echemendía	.	20	"	25 "
29 Herradura.	Sixteen pirates	.	16	"	2 July.
July.					
1 Tunicú.	Two rebels	.	2	"	5 "
3 Banao.	Two "	.	2	"	17 "
5 Herradura.	Twenty-nine pirates	.	29	"	13 "
9 Yariguá.	Andres Nuñez	.	1	"	2 Aug.
" Junco.	A rebel	.	1	"	2 "
10 Caimito.	Two rebels	.	2	"	1 "
" Domingo.	Two "	.	2	"	" "
" Loreto.	Two "	.	2	"	" "
" Guayacanes.	Two "	.	2	"	" "
15 Caimito.	José Cambra, Florentino Acosta and José Guzman	.	3	"	24 July.
" Guayamar.	Two rebels	.	2	"	30 "
" Cuba.	Four pirates of the Fannie		4	"	30 "
18 Monzon.	Capt. Francisco Pavon	.	1	"	1 Aug.
20 Ranchuelo.	One rebel	.	1	"	16 "
" Laguna Blanca.	One "		1	"	" "
" Cascajales.	Two "		2	"	" "
23 Africano.	One "		1	".	1 "
" Jarahncca.	One "		1	"	" "
" Toro.	Three "		3	"	" "
25 Cuba.	Twenty-three pirates		23	"	30 July.
26 Matecuba.	Three rebels		3	"	1 Aug.
28 Caimanes.	Two "		2	."	16 "
" Canuao.	Two "		2	"	16 "
August.					
3 Neiva.	Three "	.	3	D.	" "
" San Pablo.	" "	.	3	"	" "

2767

			2767		
30 Holguin.	Four sick in hospital	.	4	D.	5 Sep.
September.					
13 Guia.	Eight rebels	.	8	"	15 Oct.
16 Viajacas.	One "	.	1	"	29 Sep.
" Camajuaní.	Two "	.	2	"	29 "
" Banao.	One "	.	1	"	29 "
27 Potrerillo.	N. Reyes and N. Bovino		2	"	15 "
October.					
3 Mamcy.	I. A. Rojas	.	1	"	15 Oct.
6 Caimito.	Pedro G. Quiola, P. Guevara,				
	C. Rojas	.	3	"	14 Nov.
10 Remedios.	Alejandro del Rio	.	1	"	15 Oct.
13 Dátil.	Jesús Mena	.	1	"	31 "
18 Monte Verde.	One man	.	1	"	31 "
25 Veguita.	One rebel	.	1	"	31 "
27 Las Túnas.	Ramon Belisario	nother	2	"	31 "
November.					
8 San Gerónimo.	One rebel		1	"	16 Nov
" San Andrés.	Esteban Varona		1	"	16 "
December.					
15 Manicaragua.	José Gonzales	.	1	"	16 Jan.
23 Camagüey.	One rebel	.	1	"	16 "
" Cuba.	Five rebels	.	5	"	16 "
" Laguna.	One rebel	.	1	"	31 "

1873.

January.					
22 Remedios.	N. Araña	.	1	"	12 "
" Gibara.	One rebel	.	1	"	16 "
February.					
6 Guisa.	Two rebels	.	2	"	16 "
" Campano.	One "	.	1	"	" "
15 Diff. places.	Five "	.	5	"	2 Mch.
16 Sitio.	One "	.	1	"	2 "
March.					
2 Vueltas.	One rebel	.	1	"	1 Apr.
2 Sn. Fernando.	Two "	.	2	"	11 "
15 Victoria.	One "	.	1	"	19 Mar.
" Diff. places.	Two "	.	2	"	1 Apr.
23 Najasa.	Vicente Viamonte	.	1	"	1 Mch.

			2826		

April.		2826		
5 Gnáimaro.	Juan Ramirez Aldama .	1	D.	16 Apr.
15 Diff. places.	Marcial Garcia and two more	3	"	1 May.
24 Gibaro.	Antonio Cruz .	1	"	23 "
May.				
16 Camagüey.	Hilario Mendoza	1	"	18 "
June.				
29 Vapor.	Three working men .	3	"	18 July.
" Tutela.	One rebel .	1	"	24 "
July.				
7 Amero.	Two rebels .	2	D.	18 "
20 Juan Criollo.	Two rebels .	2	"	17 "
August.				
5 San Cárlos.	Six runners	6	D.	9 Aug.
13 Caobillas.	Pedro Nolasco Zayas	1	"	30 "
September.				
8 Dos Camioes.	Capt. José Maria Avila .	2	D.	14 Sept
9 Cienaga.	Two rebels .	2	"	28 "
" Ojo. de Agua.	Two " .	2	"	30 "
16 Negros.	One " .	1	"	30 "
27 Gloria.	Two " .	2	"	30 "
November.				
4 Santiago.	GENERALS BERNABE DE VARONA AND W. C. RYAN, COLONELS JESUS DEL SOL AND PEDRO CESPEDES .	4	D.	7 Nov
5 Santa Clara.	Two rebels .	2	"	11 "
6 Pulgas.	Four rebels .	4	"	15 "
7 Santiago.	Captain, José Fry ; Pilot, William Baward ; Mate, James Flood ; Sailors—J. C. Harris, John Bosa, B. P. Chamberlain, William Kose, Ignacio Dueñas, Antonio Deloyo, José Manuel Teiran, Ramon Larramendi, Eusebio Gariza, Edward Day, J. S. Trujillo, Jack Williamson, Porfirio Corvison, P. Alfaro, Thomas Crigg, Frank Good, Paul Khunrer,			

2868

			2868		
	Barney Herrald, Samuel Card, John Brown, Alfred Haisell, W. J. Price, George Thomas, Ezekiel Durham, Thomas Walter Williams, Simon Broyeur, Leopold Larose, A. Arci, John Stewart, Henry Bond, George Thompson, James Samuel, Henry Frank, James Read	37	D.	15 Nov.
8 Santiago.	Arturo Loret Mola, Agustin Varona, Oscar Varona, Guillermo Valls, José Boitel, Salvador Penedo, Enrique Castellanos, Augustin Santa Rosa, Justo Consuegra, Francisco Porras Pita, José Otero, Herminio Quesada	12	"	15 "
9 San. Manuel.	Two rebels	2	"	" "
10 Lagunas.	One rebel	1	"	" "
" Saramaguacan.	Fernando Molino, Juan Perez, Antonio Pages	3	"	" "
" Caridad.	Rafael Armas	1	"	" "
" Diff. places.	Juan Garces and two others	3	"	" "

2927

All those marked with an asterisk, have been shot in the roads when conducted to the cities for trial.

Since commencing the printing of this book we have received papers from Havana, in which we find that a large number of Cuban prisoners captured in the assault of Manzanillo, and seventeen "conspirators" in Holquin, have been shot. We have not had an opportunity to ascertain the dates or number of these last executions in time for publication.

Since the month of June, 1871, the Havana papers give only very few notices about the executions of Cubans and the *Voz de Cuba* stated that they must not be published because they would be new facts for another "Book of Blood." The number of executions is exceedingly greater and we will publish them in a supplement with the remainder of those killed in 1873.

D. means *Diario de la Marina*, organ of the Spanish Naval service.

V. de C. means *Voz de Cuba*, organ of the Spanish Volunteers.

PRISONERS

Captured by the Spaniards and whose fate has never been made known.

1869.

March.

1	Sti. Spiritus.	Four cartridge makers .	4	V. de C.	4 Mch.
2	Jaguey.	N. Sardiña . . .	1	Diario.	14 "
8	Gueiba.	Seven prisoners . .	7	"	12 "
9	Peralejo.	Eight " . .	8	"	3 Apri'.
12	Sto. Domingo.	A mulatto spy . .	1	"	16 Mch.
14	Moron.	Eleven spies . . .	11	"	29 "
15	Manzanillo.	Fifteen prisoners . .	15	"	3 Apr.
19	Sti.-Spiritus.	Two " . .	2	"	6 "
24	Guamutas.	Forty-three " . .	43	"	23 "
25	Sto. Domingo.	Six " . .	6	"	1 "
27	Niguas.	Nine " . .	9	"	23 "
29	Aserradero.	Four " . .	3	"	10 "
—	Guamutas.	Twenty-three more .	23	"	23 "
—	Mayari.	Forty " . .	40	"	16 Mch.
—	Cienfuegos.	Twenty-one" . .	21	"	19 "

April.

1	Guaracabuya.	Two prisoners . .	2	"	9 Apr.
5	Potrerillo.	Three " . . .	3	"	16 "
13	"	One spy . . .	1	"	16 "
10	"	Nine rebel chiefs . .	9	"	16 "
10	Manzanillo.	One spy . . .	1	"	22 May.
10	Jagua.	Nine prisoners . .	9	"	13 "
17	Las Lajas.	Bernardo Bonet R. C. .	1	"	22 Apr.
23	Sta. Clara.	Manuel Rojas R. C. .	1	"	28 "
23	Yaguaramas.	Antonio Moreira . .	1	"	27 May.
28	Sta. Clara.	Ricardo Ledon and Juan Lopez R. C. . .	2	"	3 "
30	Cuba.	Nine plunderers . .	9	"	7 "
—	Mayajiguas.	A number of prisoners .	5	"	7 "

May.

1	Camarones.	Four prisoners . .	4	"	7 "
9	Arimao.	Andres Diaz and one spy	2	"	15 "
15	Vasquez.	Two prisoners . .	2	"	11 Sept.
15	Tunas.	Three prisoners . .	3	"	17 June.
17	Cienfuegos.	Ant. Figueroa and N. Mesa.	2	"	20 "

252

18	Hatillo.	Thirteen from Figueredo's band	13	D.	29 May.
18	Guaracabulla.	Sacramento Carvajal, B. Machado, R. Jimenez and his two sons . . .	5	"	8 "
18	Manzanillo.	Four prisoners . .	4	"	9 "
24	Lajas.	Seven prisoners . .	7	"	2 June.
26	Nipe.	One corporal and four soldiers . . .	5	"	9 "
26	Moron.	Many prisoners . .	10	"	1 "

June.

10	Sta. Clara.	Five prisoners . .	5	"	22 "
20	Jutinicú.	One " . . .	1	"	7 July.
20	Guisa.	Ten " cap. by Boet.	10	"	8.9 "
26	Baracoa.	Eighteen" . . .	18	"	13.14 "
28	Palmira.	Seven " . . .	7	"	1 "
—	Sta. Cruz.	Four " . . .	4	"	30 June.

July.

6	Caunao.	Pio Hernandez and two more	3	"	11 July.
12	Sta. Clara.	Three spies . . .	3	"	19 Aug.
18	Barrancas.	Two prisoners . .	2	"	5 "
22	Cuba.	Three " . . .	3	"	3 "
22	Jiguaní.	One " . . .	1	"	12 "
—	Trinidad.	Three recruiting officers	3	"	30 July.
—	Caibarien.	Some prisoners . .	5	"	15 Aug.

August.

6	Palma Soriano.	Four prisoners . .	4	"	13 "
8	Sti. Spiritus.	Three " . .	3	"	17 "
11	Limones.	Four " . .	4		
11	Cachaza	Four " . .	4	"	22 "
12	Limones.	Two " . .	2	"	25 "
13	Bajadas.	Three " . .	3	"	1 Sept.
13	Cuba.	Eleven " . .	11	"	19 Aug.
14	Puerto Padre.	Three " . .	3	"	22 "
17	Hicotea.	José de J. Garcia and another	2	"	24 "
18	Baire.	Thirteen . . .	13	"	27 "
18	Cienfuegos.	Gregorio Hernandez .	1	"	20 "
19	Jibacoa.	Six prisoners . .	6	"	10 Sept.
20	Biajará.	A certain number .	5	"	1 "
20	Arroyo Blanco.	Six prisoners . .	6	"	2 "
24	Taguayabon.	Eleven . . .	11	"	1 "
24	Cubitas.	Fourteen . . .	14	"	1 "
25	Pto. Principe.	Thirteen . . .	13	"	31 Aug.
26	Central Dept.	Four by the Civiles .	4	"	29 "
28	Guines.	Nine	9	"	29 "
29	Cienfuegos.	Two	2	"	12 Sept.

483

				483		
30	Sidonia.	Three	. .	3	D.	12 Sept.
—	Sagua.	Eight	. .	8	"	29 Aug.

September.

1	Caguas.	More than fifty prisoners		51	"	10 Sept.
4	Mangas.	Twenty-four conspirators		24	"	8 "
6	San Cristobal.	Fifteen	" .	15	"	11 "
7	Cauto del Paso.	Thirty-seven (Boet)	.	37	"	9 Oct.
20	Cárdenas.	N. Macario y N. Lugo	.	2	"	26 Sept.
21	Tunas.	Juan Sancho, two more and his personal guard	.	8	"	9 Oct.
27	Jagua.	Thirteen prisoners	.	13	"	8 "
20	Las Minas.	One	. . .	I	"	12 "

October.

6	Sierra Jumagua.	Com. Mendoza and others		3	"	8 "
7	Las Lajas.	Seventy-one prisoners	.	71	"	12 "
8	Sti. Spiritus.	One	" .	1	"	14 "
10	Remedios.	One	" .	1	"	17 "
10	Puerto Padre.	Two	" .	2	"	26 "
12	Remedios.	Two	"	2	"	17 "
18	Contramaestre.	Two	" .	2	"	13 Nov.
19	Pto. Principe.	Four	" .	4	"	29 Oct.
28	Puerto Padre.	Two chiefs and five more		7	"	23 Nov.
29	El Roble.	One	.	1	"	3 "
31	Mijialito.	One	.	1	"	11 "
—	Los Negros.	Thirteen (Boet)	.	13	"	5 "

November.

1	Baguana.	Three prisoners	. .	3	"	27 "
4	Tacajó.	Zaldivar and two more	.	3	"	27 "
4	Moron.	Captain Carvajal	. .	1	"	19 "
5	Caunao.	Three prisoners.	. .	3	"	14 "
6	Jobosi.	Seven	" . .	7	"	10 "
8	Holguin.	Five	" . .	5	"	14 "
11	El Macio.	A certain number	. .	5	"	24 "
12	Caunao.	Five	. .	5	"	14 "
14	Sta. Cruz.	Lorenzo Xiques y Estrada R.C.	1	"	20 "
14	Tuinicú.	Four prisoners	. .	4	"	21 "
15	Arroyo Blanco.	Two	" . .	2	"	22 Dec.
16	Sipiabo.	One	" . .	1	"	20 Nov.
18	Moron.	Two	" . .	2	"	26 "
18	Cabaignan.	Cepeda R. C. and eleven more	12	"	2 Dec.
19	Portillo.	Manuel Codina R. C.	.	1	"	2 "
19	Pinos Blancos.	Three prisoners	.	3	"	22 "
20	Minas.	One	" . .	1	"	28 Nov.
20	Manacas.	Five bearers of seditious proclamations	. .	5	"	21 "

818

818

22	Zayas.	Three spies . .	3	"	22 Dec.
22	Remedios.	Three rebel chiefs . .	3	"	24 "
24	Sti. Spiritus.	J. M. Abreu (incendiary)	1	"	17 "
25	Caunao.	Two prisoners . .	2	"	27 Nov.
27	Holguin.	N. Ramirez, N. Sarmiento and N. Chavarria . .	3	"	14 Dec.
28	Guá.	Angel Colas, recruiting officer	1	"	8 "
	C. de Zapata.	Ten spies . . .	10	"	2 "

December.

12	Palmira.	Three prisoners . .	3	D.	24 "
14	Velazquez.	Five " . .	5	"	30 "
14	Purial.	One " . .	1	"	6 Jan.
17	Seibabo.	Twelve " . .	12	"	26 "
21	Arroyo Blanco.	Twenty-five . .	25	"	28 Dec.
23	Bijarú.	A certain number of spies	5	"	30 "
23	Baez.	Five prisoners . .	5	"	26 Jan.
24	Holguin.	Bernardo Millares, Eladio Cabrera R. C. . .	2	"	15 "
27	Mataguan.	Sixty-seven prisoners .	67	"	1 "
27	Sti. Spiritus.	Two armed rebels .	2	"	15 "
31	Pta. de Guano.	One " .	1	"	5 "
31	Casimba.	Four " .	4	"	11 "

January.

3	Sta. Catalinai.	Four rebels . .	4	"	11 "
6	" "	Felix Ferrer . .	1	"	13 "
7	Sta. Cruz.	One rebel . .	1	"	13 "
11	Pto. del Padre.	Eight prisoners . .	8	"	25 "
12	Yaguas.	Two " . .	2	"	23 "
15	Guinia.	A certain number of prisoners	5	"	21 "
17	Limones.	Three prisoners . .	3	"	25 "
20	Cauto.	Four " . .	4	"	11 Feb.
21	Marroquin.	One chief and three more	4	"	31 Jan.
21	Sta. Clara.	Three prisoners . .	3	"	24 "
24	Holguin.	Three " . . .	3	"	29 "
24	Barajagua	Some prisoners, among them the chiefs Fernando Toro and B. Perez . .	5	"	30 "
24	Palmarejo.	One prisoner . .	1	"	5 Feb.
24	El Roble.	One " . .	1	"	27 Jan.
24	Cubitas.	Two " . .	2	"	11 Feb.
25	Caunaito.	Six " . .	6	"	29 Jan.
20 to 28	Pto. Princ.	Twenty-eight prisoners .	28	"	8 Feb.

· 1,054

1,054

February.

1	Pto. Príncipe.	Twenty-three more prisoners 23	D.	3 Feb.
3	" "	Seven more "	7 "	8 "
4	Yayabo.	One incendiary . .	1 "	11 "
6	Los Guerreros.	Seven prisoners . .	7 "	11 "
7	Sevilla.	Tomas Martinez & two more 3 "		17 "
8	Pto. Príncipe.	Ten prisoners . .	10 "	15 "
10	Bagá.	Nine more . .	9 "	13 "

February
22	Cambuto.	Seven prisoners . .	7 "	8 Mch.
23	El Ramon.	One " . .	1 "	3 "
23	Cascorro.	Zacarias Diaz, Agustin Llanes and Nicolas Montero 3 "		15 "
24	Santo Spiritus.	Two incendiaries . .	2 "	1 "
25	Las Minas.	Six prisoners . .	6 "	2 "
28	Santo Spiritus.	Three " . .	3 "	2 "

March.
3	San Luis.	Nine prisoners . .	9 "	10 "
3	El Jumento.	One " . .	1 "	1 Apr.
5	Cambite.	Three captured by Boet 3 "		12 Mch.
7	Guinia.	Three prisoners . .	3 "	15 "
6 to 8	Holguin.	Four " . .	4 "	12 "
1 to 9	Aguas Verdes.	Many prisoners . .	10 "	12 "
1 to 5	Cobre.	Soma captured by Boet 5 "		12 "
10	Peñagorda.	One prisoner . .	1 "	1 "
10	Guanajayabo.	Two " . .	2 "	3 "
10	Purial.	Two " . .	2 "	3 "
11	Manicaragua.	One " . .	1 "	17 "
14	Seiba.	Four " . .	4 "	29 "
16	Canto.	Seven " . .	7 "	25 "
17	Congreso.	Three " . .	3 "	24 "
22	Canto.	Thirty-six captured by Boet 36 "		8 Apr.
23	Pto. Príncipe.	Three prisoners . .	3 "	27 Mch.
25	Santa Clara.	Three "	3 "	29 "
27	Maniabon.	Eight "	8 "	5 "

April.
1	Las Parras.	Eight, among them some chiefs 8 "		16 "
3	Pto. Príncipe.	Six prisoners . .	6 "	14 "
4	Magarabomba.	Four " . .	4 "	21 "
5	Caunao.	Six " . .	6 "	8 "
5	Santi Spiritus.	Three " . .	3 "	12 "
8	Cacatual.	One " . .	1 "	14 "
8	Sabanilla.	Two prisoners . .	2 "	99 Apr.
11	Guira.	One " . .	1 "	13 "
11	Ojo de Agua.	Nine " . .	9 "	20 "

1,281

			1,281			
12	Santi Spiritus.	Twenty-four conspirators who aided the rebels	24	D.	16 Apr.
13	Cannao.	Four rebels	4	"	14 "
14	Uruguay.	One letter carrier and twenty-one prisoners captured by Boet	22	"	26 "
15	Pto. Naranjo.	Four rebels in arms	4	"	26 "
17	Gibara.	Commander Juan Sales and Pablo Luis Villegas	2	"	26 "
17	Holguin.	Five rebels from Peralta's band	5	"	30 "
18	Mamanayagua.	Thirty prisoners	30	"	24 "
18	Calesito.	Two "	2	"	24 "
18	Holguin.	Nine "	9	"	30 "
18	Moron.	Sixteen "	16	"	2 May.
21	Cayo Loco.	One "	1	"	14 Apr.
21	Yaguajay.	One "	1	"	26 "
21	Trinidad.	Chief Man. Rodriguez, Francisco and José Diaz	3	"	26 "
24	Cannao.	Prefect Betancourt, & twelve men	13	"	27 "
24	Cubitas.	One hundred and thirty-six	136	" .	27 "
25	Guanaja.	One prisoner	1	"	1 May.
18 to 25	Las Sierras.	Six "	6	"	2 "
27	Pto. Principe.	Thirteen prisoners	13	"	2 "
27 to 29	"	Six "	6	"	17 "
30	" "	Eleven "	11	"	1 "
30	La Matilde.	Four "	4	"	10 "
27 to 7 May	Pto. Principe.	Twenty-one prisoners of Montaner	21	"	17 "

May.

1	Cano.	Some rebels manufacturing gunpowder	5	"	4 "
1	Guara.	One with arms	1	"	4 "
2	Arroyo Bermejo.	Three prisoners	3	"	4 "
4	Trinidad.	Twenty-five members of a Junta	25	"	6 "
2 to 5	Santa Clara.	Seven prisoners	7	"	6 "
5	Nuevitas.	Seven rebel chiefs	7	"	8 "
9	Caoba.	One prisoner	1	"	12 "
11	Yaguajay.	One rebel prisoner	1	"	13 "
11	Remedios.	Five " "	5	"	14 "
11	Arroyon.	One " "	1	"	19 "
11	Palopicado.	One " "	1	"	18 "
12	Bicana.	One " "	1	"	25 "
14	Maraguan.	Nine " "	9	"	22 "

16,82

			1,682		
14	Ciego de Najaza.	Nineteen prisoners .	19	D.	24 May.
18	Moron.	One " .	1	"	22 "
18	Monte Oscuro.	Nine " .	9	"	1 June.
18	Calento.	One " .	1	"	22 May.
11 to 18 Pto. Prin- cipe.		Twenty-two mo e captured Montaner . .	22	"	2 June.
11 to 18 " "		Seventeen by Chinchilla	17	"	3 "
19	Santa Clara.	Two prisoners .	2	"	29 Ma .
22	Pto. Principe.	Twenty-two more .	22	"	22 "
22	Sagua.	Paulino Yeros, José Rodriguez and Matias Pavon .	3	"	29 "
4	Vista Hermosa.	Many prisoners .	10	"	8 June.
6	Guajabana.	One " .	1	"	1 "
26	Aserradero.	Three " .	3	"	10 "
27	Punta Brava.	Six " .	6	"	8 "
30	Maraguan.	Thirty " .	30	"	3 "
31	Caimanera.	One " .	1	"	3 "
—	Holguin.	Nine " .	9	"	1 "
—	Puerto Princi- pe.	Seventy-nine rebels captured by three combined co- lumns . .	79	"	14 "

June.

2	Limones.	Eight prisoners .	8	"	16 "
2	Divertido.	Four " .	4	"	7 "
9	Ciénaga.	Chief Pablo Recio and one mulato . .	2	"	16 "
8	San Miguel.	Six rebels . .	6	"	14 "
11	Najaza.	Six " . .	6	"	17 "
11	Yaguajay.	Three " . .	3	"	20 "
17	Baga.	One " . .	1	"	5 July.
17	Seibabo.	One " . .	1	"	7 "
18	Cauto.	Forty " . .	40	"	24 June.
18	Bayamo.	Four " . .	4	"	" " .

June.

18	Vertientes.	Pablo Barrios, Prefect Fer- nando Varona, José J. Fer- nandez and two more	5	"	29 Jun.
22	Voladores.	Nineteen prisoners .	19	"	24 "
22	Pto. Principe.	Sixteen " .	16	"	26 "
22	Palmar.	One " .	1	"	29 "
22	Guayabo.	One " .	1	"	7 July.
20	Pto. Principe.	Twenty-seven captured in different incursions	27	"	30 June.

July.

7	Yareyal.	One prisoner .	1	"	10 July.

2,072

			2,072		
7	Las Lajas.	Three prisoners	3	D.	28 July.
7	Quemados.	One "	1	"	11 "
7	Pto. Principe.	Nine "	9	"	12 "
8	Aguada.	One "	1	"	19 "
9	Vista Hermosa.	Seventeen wounded and ten more	27	"	17 "
9	Jiguaní.	Fifteen prisoners	15	"	20 "
12	Santa Cruz.	Bernabé Morales, and his son Eduardo, Juan Sanchez, Jose Arce, and Ramon Varona	5	"	21 "
5	Tibisial	Two prisoners	2	"	22 "
0	Muragua.	Eleven captured by Montaner	11	"	28 "
22	Yaguajay.	Prefect B. Gareño	1	"	28 "
22	Santa Cruz.	Twenty-three rebels, among them six prominent persons	23	"	29 "
24	Yaguajay.	Two prisoners	2	"	28 "
26	La Gloria.	Two "	2	"	14 Aug.

August.

8	Guaní	Juan Ferrer, Pedro Rios, and three more	5	"	10 Aug.
24	Arroyo Blanco.	Rafael Peralta	1	"	2 Sept.
--	Cuba.	Six prisoners	6	"	2 "
28	Caunao.	Fifteen "	15	"	7 "
31	Villas.	Five "	5	"	3 "
31	Pto. Principe.	One "	1	"	3 "
—.	Manzanillo.	Eleven captured in different incursions	11	"	9 "
7	Pto. Principe.	Twenty-two prisoners	22	"	14 "
7	Holguin.	Three "	3	"	27 "
10	Deseada.	Two "	2	"	3 Oct.
11	Guanausi.	Four "	4	"	3 "
17	Yareyal.	Two "	2	"	3 "
20	Guaimaro.	Twelve "	12	"	1 "
25	Sti. Spiritus.	Two "	2	"	29 Sept.
30	Holguin.	One "	1	"	18 Oct.

October.

2	Quemadito.	Seventy-five wounded	75	"	16 "
3	Sti. Spiritus.	One prefect	1	"	5 "
5	"	One letter carrier	1	"	28 "
7	Remedios.	The father-in-law of Boitel, and another	2	"	16 "
8	Hi otea.	One prisoner	1	"	16 "

2,346

					2,343	
11	Gua.	Three prisoners	.	3	D.	27 Oct.
12	La Deseada.	Five "	.	5	"	26 "
16	Trinidad.	One "	.	1	"	25 "
19	Tacamara.	José Carvajal and his son		2	"	6 Nov.
20	Yareyal.	José Martinez, and four more	5	"	6 "
2?	Remedios.	Pedro Garcia and Agustin				
		Ramirez . .	2	"	8 "
23	Santa Clara.	One prisoner	.	1	"	27 Oct.
13	La Deseada.	Seven " . .	7	"	1 Nov.
16	Majaguas.	Two " . .	2	"	4 "
16	Pirindingo.	Eleven " . .	11	"	1 "
27	Yara.	Three " . .	3	"	9 "
19	Charco Azul.	Six (two of them chiefs)	6	"	4 "
29	Central Dept.	Three captured in some incur-				
		sions . .	3	"	9 "

November.

1	Las Parras.	Four prisoners	.	4	"	16 Nov.
2	El Rosario.	Nazario Rodriguez Feo	1	"	4 "
2	C. de Zapata.	Some prisoners	.	5	"	8 "
2	Yagruma.	One "	.	1	"	8 "
2	Vista Hermosa.	Eight "	.	8	"	2 Dec.
2	Central Dept.	Five cap'd in some incursions	5	D.	13 Nov.
3	Pto. Principe.	One prefect	.	1	"	15 "
5	Sti. Spíritus.	Manuel Barrera	.	1	"	3 "
5	Arroyo Blanco.	Four . .	4	"	13 "
6	Sta. Isabel.	Felix Duret . .	1	"	16 "
6	Banao.	Six . .	6	"	20 "
10	Sti. Spíritus.	Six . .	6	"	15 "
11	Colon.	Juan Vera . .	1	"	15 "
13	Potrerillo.	Three prisoners	.	3	"	22 "
13	Maniabon.	Juan Serrano and Luis Ra-				
		mirez . .	2	"	2 Dec.
17	Salado.	Three prisoners	.	3	"	17 "
17	Limones.	One prisoner wounded	1	"	17 "
17	Tempú.	Four " . .	4	"	27 Nov.
17	Esperanza.	Two " . .	2	"	24 "
18	Jiguaní.	M. Villareal, his brother and				
		three more .	5	"	2 Dec.
18	Canasi.	Three prisoners	.	3	"	11 "
19	Guaimaro.	Ten prisoners captured in				
		some incursions .	10	"	1 "
22	Yaguaramas,	One prisoner , ,	1	"	27 Nov,
22	Paredones.	Six " , ,	6	"	1 Dec,
22	La Cueva,.	Two " . ,	2	"	6 "
23	Jaguey Gde.	Two " . .	2	"	3 "
24	Cubitas,	Two " , .	2	"	1 "

2,487

			2,487				
26	Tavira.	One prisoner .	1	D.	3	Dec.	
28	——	One rebel cap. by the civil g'rd	1	"	3	"	
28	Canasí.	Thirteen cap. in diff. excurs'ns	13	"	11	"	
—	Las Tunas.	Admiral (?) Nuñez & five more	6	"	6	"	

December.

1	Cienfuegos.	Manuel Gonzales .	1	"	17	"
2	Tuero.	Two rebels . .	2	"	8	"
7	Farallones	Rafael Cepeda .	1	"	13	"
9	Los Cristales.	Three prisoners .	3	"	14	"
9	Sti-Spíritus.	Fourteen " .	14	"	17	"
9	Las Lomas.	Prefect José Conesa, Cap. Sosé G. Luna and three more	5	"	10	"
9	El Jumento.	Five prisoners .	5	"	17	"
9	Zapata.	Four rebels .	4	D.	16	"
10	St. Spíritu.	Three " . .	3	"	16	"
10	"	Seventeen rebels .	17	"	21	"
11	Quemado.	Two " .	2	"	21	"
12	Trinidad.	José Leonardo Ortega	1	"	20	"
12	Jiquí.	Ten rebels .	10	"	27	"
18	Pto. Príncipe.	Eighteen rebels .	18	"	1	Jan.
19	Remedios.	Four " .	4	"	23	Dec.
23	Almazan.	Three " .	3	"	15	Jan.
27	Pto. Príncipe.	Thirty-four captured in different excursions .	34	"	7	"
29	Villas.	Three . .	3	"	4	"
30	Guanaja.	Juan C. Zenea ,	1	"	14	"
31	Santa Clara.	One rebel . .	1	"	3	"
—	Vis. Hermosa.	Ten . .	10	"	20	"

1871.

January.

1	Vergel.	A prisoner .	1	D.	4	Jan.
"	St. Agustin.	" .	1	"	"	"
"	Monte Alto.	" .	1	"	"	"
"	Camagüey.	Manuel Castellanos .	1	"	"	"
"	Sti. Espíritu.	Seventeen prisoners .	17	"	6	"
"	Camagüey.	Lope Recio Agramonte, Rafael Cotrino and eight others	10	"	7	"
"	"	Twenty-four prisoners .	24	"	"	"
"	"	Eighteen prisoners .	8	"	"	"
"	Sti. Espíritu.	A prisoner .	1	"	10	"
"	Scibabo.	Two " .	2	"	15	"
"	Corojo.	A negro .	1	"	"	"
2	Guanaja.	Emilio Torres and six others	7	"	14	"

			2734

		2734		
4 Guanaja.	Four prisoners	4	D.	14 Jan.
10 Cienfuegos.	Seven rebels	7	"	13 "
12 Cascorro.	A prisoner	1	"	11 Feb.
13	Twenty from the Hornet expedition	20	"	19 Jan.
15 Sti. Espíritu.	Four prisoners	4	"	20 "
" Camagüey.	Ten prisoners	10	"	" "
" Güinia de Miranda	Tomas Diaz	1	"	29 "
" Mate.	Benigno Tamayo and eighteen others	19	"	15 Feb.
" Holguin.	Two prisoners	2	D.	29 Jan.
20 Cascorro.	"	2	"	" "
27 Sti. Espíritu.	One "	1	"	8 Feb.
29 Ciego de Avila.	A postman and two rebels.	3	"	17 Mar.
30 Sti. Espíritu.	Two prisoners.	2	"	8 Feb.
" Guaimaro.	"	2	"	11 Feb.
" Camagüey.	Cristobal Diaz	1	"	" "
31 Minas.	Manuel Castro and four others	5	"	" "
" Santiago.	Eighteen prisoners	18	"	3 "
" Pto. Príncipe.	Fifteen "	15	"	" "

February.

2 Pto. Príncipe.	Three prisoners	3	D.	11 Feb.
" Cascorro.	Five "	5	"	14 "
6 Margaritá.	Five "	5	"	24 "
" Cuba.	Two "	2	"	" "
" San Jorge.	" "	2	"	" "
6 Cinco Villas.	Major Leopoldo Villegas	1	D.	4 Mar.
" Siguanea.	Carlos Cerveceño	1	"	" "
" Nicho.	One prisoner	1	"	8 Feb.
" Buena Vista.	"	1	"	" "
7 San Gerónimo.	"	1	"	4 Mar.
8 Tunas.	"	1	"	23 Feb.
"	Nicolas Govin	1	"	17 Mch
9 Sti. Espíritu.	One prisoner	1	"	15 Feb.
16 "	N. Marin	1	"	24 "
" Jumento.	Three prisoners	3	"	" "
17 Divertido.	Two "	2	"	" "
" Corojal.	Two "	2	"	" "
" Bayamo.	Three "	3	"	" "
23 Camagüey.	Clemente Sosa, Provost Sergeant Callejas and L. Miranda	3	"	12 Mch
" St. Miguel.	One mulatto and a negro	2	"	" "
24 Guaimarillo.	Rafael Palomares and his son	2	"	17 "
" Laguno.	One prisoner	1	"	" "
27 "	Manuel Rojas and Juan C. Silverio	2	"	4 "

2897

			2897		
28 Ciego de Avila.	Two rebels	.	2	D.	10 Mch.
" Pto. Príncipe.	Five prisoners	.	5	"	" "
" Pilar.	One negro and one white man		2	"	17 "
28 Baños.	Two prisoners	.	2	"	17 "
" Different places.	Fifteen "	.	15	"	" "

March.

3 Camagüey.	Constantino Agüero	.	1	D	12 Mch.
" Cinco Villas.	One prisoner	.	1	"	30 "
" Caunao.	F. Rodriguez Fernandez	.	1	"	15 "
" Carraguao.	One prisoner	.	1	"	17 "
7 Angeles.	One "	.	1	"	" "
7 Sti. Espíritu.	Four "	.	4		" "
10 "	Seven "	.	7	"	" "
" Camaguey.	N. Huelva and three others		4	"	" "
11 Villa Clara.	Three rebels	.	3	"	" "
16 Canoa.	One prisoner	.	1	"	19 "
17 Barajagua.	Two prisoners	.	2	"	28 "
18 Palmira.	One "	.	1	"	" "
18 Camagüey.	E. Nuñez and F. Zayas	.	2	"	31 "
20 Puercro.	Two prisoners	.	2	"	30 "
21 Camagüey.	J. J. Cosio	.	1	"	· 30 "
23 Cabezas.	Some prisoners	.	3	"	18 Apr.
25 Mefan.	One " "	.	1	"	" "
26 Barrancas.	One "	.	1	"	" "
" Palma.	A young man	.	1	"	" "
29 Guaimaro.	Two rebels	.	2	"	30 "
31 Barajaguas.	One rebel	.	1	"	16 "
" Trinidad.	One rebel	.	1	"	" "

April.

4 Mefan.	One prisoner	.	1	D.	16 Apr.
" Quimado.	One "	.	1	"	" "
" Remanga Enagua	Three prisoners	.	3	"	" "
5 S. Lorenzo.	One prisoner	.	1	"	24 "
11 Mayajiguas.	Three prisoners	.	3	"	30 "
12 Trinidad.	Eight prisoners	.	8	"	18 "
19 Demajagua.	One prisoner	.	1	"	30 "
20 Ti Arriba.	Two prisoners	.	2	"	" "
21 Sti. Espírita.	Justo Llanos and 6 others		7	"	" "
23 Santiago,	Roque Trujillo	,	1	"	" "
" Cobre,	Seven prisoners	,	7	"	" "
25 Guinia	One prisoner	.	1	"	" "
" Sti. Espíritu.	One lieutenant and another		2	"	" "
29 Cadiz.	One prisoner	,	1	"	2 May,

3004

May.

			3004		
3 Arroyo Blanco.	One prisoner	.	1	D.	4 May.
" Cuba.	Fourteen prisoners	.	14	"	4 "
" Guasimal.	One prisoner	.	1	"	7 "
5 Nuevitas.	Fifteen prisoners	.	15	"	8 "
6 Moron.	Four prisoners	.	4	"	13 "
13 Sti. Espíritu.	Six prisoners	.	6	"	" "
15 Centro.	Nineteen prisoners	.	19	"	16 "
16 Güira.	Four prisoners	.	4	D.	16 June
" Pinalito.	Two prisoners	.	2	"	" "
" Cauto.	Three prisoners	.	3	"	" "
22 Desuello.	One prisoner	.	1	"	22 "
25 Yayguajay.	Three prisoners	.	3	"	17 "
" Sti. Espíritu.	Twenty-one prisoners	.	21	"	31 May.
26 Vicios.	Eight prisoners	.	8	"	14 June
" Pto. Príncipe.	Four prisoners	.	4	"	4 "
27 Moron.	Eighteen prisoners	.	18	"	16 "
31 Ramblazo.	Nine prisoners	.	9	"	9 "
" Manga Larga.	Three prisoners	.	3	"	16 "

June.

2 Cauto Abajo.	Two prisoners	.	2	D.	1 July
3 Moron.	Two prisoners	.	2	"	16 June
4 B juquero.	One prisoner	.	1	"	1 July
5 Pto. Príncipe.	Guillermo Porro	.	1	"	16 June
6 Vertientes.	Two prisoners	.	2	"	14 "
8 Perú.	Five prisours	.	5	"	" "
11 Cayo Cruz.	Felipe Vacqué	.	1	"	21 July.
" Sti. Espíritu.	Thirteen prisoners	.	13	"	17 "
14 Moron.	One rebel	.	1	"	1 "
15 Camajuaní.	Two rebels	.	2	"	24 June
" Jiquima.	Two rebels	.	2	"	1 July
16 Mulato.	Seven rebels	.	7	"	30 June
" Najaza.	Two armed children, 13 years old, not shot, notwithstanding they were rebel soldiers.	.	2	"	30 "
16 Jíbaro.	Four rebels	.	4	"	1 July
17 Najaza.	Fourteen rebels	.	14	"	30 June
" St. Clara.	Four rebels	.	4	"	1 July.
18 Trinidad.	Twenty-one rebels	.	21	"	27 June
19 Moron.	Three rebels	.	3	"	1 July.
" Manacas.	One rebel	.	1	"	24 June
" Sti. Espíritu.	Three rebels	.	3	"	27 "
22 Cabaniguan.	Two rebels	.	2	"	1 July.
24 Tunas.	Two rebels	.	2	"	18 "
25 Santero.	Gregorio Ruiz	.	1	"	4 "
27 Moron.	Five rebels	.	5	"	8 "

3241

			3241		
31 Playuela.	Fourteen rebels	.	14	D.	1 July.
31 Guaimaro.	Eight rebels	.	8	"	1 "
July.					
1 Santa Clara.	W. Feo	.	1	D.	20 July.
2 Loreto.	Two prisoners	.	2	"	19 "
3 Capestani.	One prisoner	.	11	"	8 "
" Manzanillo.	Three prisoners	.	3	"	19 "
4 Arroyo Blanco.	Six prisoners	.	6	"	12 "
" Trinidad.	Three prisoners	.	3	"	11 "
" Manzanillo.	David Baldaquin	.	1	"	" "
-8 Yaguajay.	Two prisoners	.	2	"	20 "
9 Cascorro.	Two prisoners	.	2	"	19 "
11 Júcaro.	Three prisoners	.	3	"	18 "
Tana.	Seven prisoners	.	7	"	1 Aug.
12 Dajao.	One chinaman	.	1	"	13 July.
Bayamo.	Two prisoners	.	2	"	14 "
Sti. Espíritu.	Eight prisoners	.	8	"	25 "
14 Jobo.	Seven prisoners	.	7	"	28 "
" Camajuani.	One rebel	.	1	"	1 Aug.
" Alegria.	Six prisoners	.	6	"	" "
" Piedras.	One prisoner	.	1	"	" "
15 Santa Rosa.	Fifteen prisoners	.	15	"	" "
17 Muñoz.	One prisoner	.	1	"	16 "
" Holguin.	One prisoner	.	1	"	11 "
18 Santa Clara.	Seven prisoners	.	7	"	30 July.
" Güira.	One prisoner	.	1	"	20 "
19 Santa Ana.	D. Olivet and 6 others	.	7	"	25 "
" Cuevas	One prisoner	.	1	"	1 Aug.
20 Santi Espíritu.	Five prisoners	.	5	"	1 "
22 Matanzas.	Manuel Alvarez, Domingo Hernandez, Fabian Olivera		3	"	23 July.
22 El Paso.	Four prisoners	.	4	"	1 Aug.
" Bayamo.	Carlos Quesada. and Col. Miguel Figueredo		2	"	" "
23 Sti Espíritu.	Two prisoners	.	2	"	" "
" Yayuajay.	Two prisoners	.	2	"	" "
24 Moron.	Laureano Castillo, S. Calzado, and two others		4	"	8 "
25 Pedregon.	One prisoner	.	1	"	1 "
27 Jobosi.	Eight prisoners	.	8	"	16 "
27 Palma Sola.	One prisoner	.	1	"	17 "
29 Charcas.	Col. Gustavo Figueredo	.	1	"	16 "
30 Moron.	One prisoner	.	1	"	8 "
31 Neivas.	Seven prisoners	.	7	"	8 "
" Ceiba.	Twelve prisoners	.	12	"	8 "

3417

August.

			2103			
2 Moron.	Five prisoners	.	5	"	16	"
5 Moron.	One prisoner	.	1	"	"	"
14 Palo.	Five prisoners	.	5	"	22	"
" Toro.	Five prisoners	.	5	"	26	"
" Cayo Romano.	Eduardo Barreal, José, and Eleno Cantero	.	3	"	27	"
" Salvia.	Four prisoners	.	4	"	29	"
" Tana.	Six prisoners	.	6	"	1 Sept.	
" Pto. Príncipe.	Three prisoners	.	3	"	1	"
18 Arroyo Berraco.	N. Calderin and another	.	2	"	26 Aug.	
19 Habana.	Francisco Guiral	.	1	"	20	"
20 Guaimaro.	Six prisoners	.	6	"	29	"
21 Pino Tuerto.	Three prisoners	.	3	"	31	"
23 San Pedro.	One prisoner	.	1	"	12 Sept.	
28 Nájero.	Three prisoners	.	3	"	12	"

September.

5 Nájero.	Three prisoners	.	3	D.	1 Oct.	
10 Trinidad.	Seven prisoners	.	7	"	15 Sept.	
15 Ciego de Avila.	Two prisoners	.	2	"	27	"
16 Sta. Ines.	José R. Pozo	.	1	"	7 Oct.	
" Manzanillo.	N. Chenard and two others		3	"	8	"
" Sn. Miguel.	Two prisoners	.	2	"	1	"
17 Jiguani.	One prisoner	.	1	"	17	"
" Sti. Spiritus.	Six prisoners	.	6	"	"	"
20 Veguita.	Four prisoners	.	4	"	"	"
" St. Rafael.	One prisoner	.	1	"	"	"
" Cuba.	One prisoner	.	1	"	"	"
" Veladezo.	One prisoner	.	1	"	"	"
21 Palma.	Three prisoners	.	3	"	1	"
22 San Pedro.	One prisoner	.	1	"	17	"
" Arroyo Blanco.	One prisoner	.	1	"	"	"
" Alitos.	One prisoner	.	1	"	"	"
28 Taguajai.	One prisoner	.	1	"	1	"
" Manganello.	Five prisoners	.	5	"	11	"

October.

1 Yareyal.	Antonio Fernandez	.	1	D.	15 Oct.	
" Rio Grande.	One prisoner	.	1	"	17	"
3 Altavista.	One prisoner	.	1	"	"	"
5 Linea.	Two prisoners	.	2	"	"	"
9 Guayacanes.	One prisoner	.	1	"	"	"
11 Centro.	Four prisoners	.	4	"	"	"
20 San Miguel.	Martin Barruelto y Joaquín Rodriguez	.	2	"	17 Nov.	
21 Las Tunas.	Antonio Oliva and a negro	.	1	"	14	"
23 Las Tunas.	Five prisoners	.	5	"	"	"

2213

			2213			
24 Najaza.	M. Basulto	.	1	"	3	"
" Quemado.	J. G. Molina y M. L. Revuelto	2	"	17	"
25 Pto. Príncipe.	One prisoner	.	1	"	27	"
25 Las Tunas.	Two prisoners	;	2	"	14	"
28 Las Lajas.	One prisoner	;	1	"	14	"
29 Camajuani.	Three prisoners	,	3	"	4	"
29 Mal Pais.	One prisoner	,	1	"	14	"
31 Santa Marta.	Two prisoners	,	2	"	3	"
" Cunagua.	One prisoner	.	1	"	3	"
" Hoyos.	One prisoner	.	1		17	"

November.

3 Alegria.	Seven prisoners	,	7	D.	1	Oct.
5 San Bartolo.	Two prisoners	.	2	"	"	"
5 San Joaquin.	Seven prisoners	.	7	"	"	"
6 Iguará.	One prisoner	.	1	"	17	Nov.
6 Trinidad.	One Chinaman	.	1	"	14	"
7 Ciego.	Two prisoners	.	2	"	12	"
8 Santa Fé.	One prisoner	.	1	"	17	"
8 Mamey.	A man and his two sons	.	3	"	18	"
8 Tempú.	Twelve prisoners	.	12	"	1	] c".
10 Pirindingo.	N. Castellon	.	1	"	17	Nov.
" Holguin.	A Tamayo	.	1	"	"	"
" Mijial.	Manuel Guerra and Manuel Ortiz	.	2	"	"	"
" Ventorrillo.	One man	.	1	"	"	"
" Santa Marta.	Porfirio Delgado	.	1	"	22	"
" San Gerónimo.	Seven prisoners	.	7	"	"	"
" Placeas.	One prisoner	.	1	"	23	"
" Palma Soriano.	Twenty-nine prisoners	.	29	"	1	Dec.
12 Sancti Espiritus.	Twenty prisoners	.	20	"	21	Nov.
" Crimea.	One prisoner	.	1	"	1	Dec.
" Taya.	Two prisoners	.	2	"	"	"
14 Punta Gorda.	One prisoner	.	1	"	12	"
15 La Victoria.	G. Saavedra	.	1	"	"	"
18 Santa Rosa.	One prisoner	.	1	"	"	"
19 Sti. Espíritus.	Two prisoners	.	2	"	21	Nov.
" Mendigutia.	Three prisoners	.	3	"	"	"
20 Ciego.	Seven prisoners	.	7	"	1	Dec.
" Las. Tunas.	Five prisoners	.	5	"	"	"
" Yoro.	One prisoner	.	1	"	"	"
" Presidio.	Two prisoners	.	2	"	12	"
" Trilladera.	Three prisoners	.	3	"	13	"
" Nigua.	Federico Acosta	.	1	"	1	"
23 Pelonas.	One prisoner	.	1	"	12	"
26 Tibisial.	One prisoner	.	1	"	1	"

2359

December,

			2359			
1	Diff. places.	Twelve prisoners .	12	D.	1	Dec.
"	Pto. Principe.	M. Agüero and M. Fernan'ez	2	"	17	"
2	Gomez.	Four prisoners .	4	"	6	"
3	Pilon.	One prisoner .	1	"	14	"
3	Calabera.	One prisoner .	1	"	"	"
7	Moron.	A. Rodriguez and D. Avila	2	"	29	"
9	San. Agustin.	Five prisoners	5	"	31	"
9	Melones.	Two prisoners .	2	"	"	"
11	Piedra.	A rebel boy .	1	"	30	"
"	Santiago.	N. Saavedra .	1	"	31	"
14	Jagüey.	Y. Estrada M. Barreto .				
1	"	N. Cespedes and J. Agramonte	4	"	22	"
17	Camagüey.	Four prisoners .	4	"	23	"
20	Camajaguani.	One prisoner .	1	"	22	"
"	Pto. Principe.	Three prisoners .	3	"	"	"
"	Trinidad.	One prisoner .	1	"	31	"
"	San José.	Four prisoners .	4	"	"	"
25	Holguin.	Twenty-three prisoners .	23	"	28	"
"	Soledad.	Eight prisoners	8	"	31	"
"	Prosperidad.	One prisoner .	1	"	"	"
26	Monte Grande.	Two prisoners .	2	"	12	Jan.
27	Soledad.	One prisoner .	1	'	31	"

1872.

January.

1	Jimirú.	One prisoner .	1	"	4	"
"	Seboruco.	Two prisoners .	2	"	18	"
2	"	Seven prisoners .	7	"	4	"
5	Santa Lucia.	One prisoner .	1	"	18	"
"	Cuba.	Twelve prisoners .	12	"	"	"
6	La Trocha.	One deserter .	1	"	20	"
14	Guaicanamar.	Six prisoners .	6	"	3	Feb.
21	La Cienega.	One prisoner .	1	"	16	"
"	San Miguel.	Five prisoners .	5	"	23	"
26	Guaguaco.	Six prisoners .	6	"	16	"
28	Rio Negro.	Two prisoners .	2	"	8	"
28	La Holguinera.	One prisoner .	1	"	31	Jan.

August,

3	Lugares.	One man .	1	D.	1	Mch.
7	Guamuri.	Captain Julian Arraiz and four more .	5	"	28	Feb,
7	Curana.	Seven prisoners .	7	"	"	"
12	Sabana,	One prisoner ,	1	"	23	"

2501

			2501			
13 Malograda.	Seven prisoners	.	7	"	24	"
15 Santiago.	Thirty-nine prisoners	.	39	"	16	"
18 Jagua.	Three prisoners	.	3	"	24	"
" Cambute.	One prisoner	.	1	"	"	"
21 Zaza.	José Garcia	.	1	"	25 Feb.	
" San Francisco.	Rosendo Pardo, and two others	3	"	7 Mch.	
" Chorrilio.	Seven prisoners	.	7	"	5	"
25 Guaicanamar.	Seven prisoners	.	7	"	1	"

March.

1 Las Tunas.	Twenty-three prisoners	.	1	D.	14 Mch.	
4 Jibara.	Vicente Barragan and ten more	11	"	24	"
15 Las Tunas.	Fifteen prisoners	.	15	"	31	"
" Sevilla.	P. A. Ramos and five more	6	"	"	"
18 La Veguita.	Eight prisoners	.	8	"	22	"
" Cauto.	Four prisoners	.	4	"	31	"
" Cuba.	Nine prisoners	.	9	'	31	"
27 Las Catas.	Three prisoners	.	3	"	14 Apr.	
15 El Sitio.	Three prisoners	.	3	"	"	"

April.

4 Las Tunas.	Three prisoners	.	3	D.	24 Apr.	
6 La Güira.	Three prisoners	.	3	"	"	"
11 Jaguey.	Three prisoners	.	3	"	"	"
16 Nuevitas.	Sixteen prisoners	.	16	"	"	"
15 Cuba.	Fifty-five prisoners	.	55	"	16 June.	
19 Dolores.	Twenty-three prisoners	.	23	"	12	'
30 Las Tunas.	Thirty-nine prisoners	.	39	"	1	"

May.

7 Holguin.	Four prisoners	.	4	D.	28 May.	
15 Cuba.	Seventy-three prisoners	.	73	"	16	"
30 Central Dep.	Twenty-eight prisoners	.	28	"	31	"
31 Baire.	Two prisoners	.	2	"	12 June	

June.

4 Manzanillo.	Nine prisoners	.	9	D.	6 June.	
7 Mamey.	Eleven prisoners	.	11	"	18	"
14 Guantánamo.	Twenty five prisoners	.	25	"	28	"
15 Santiago.	One hundred and forty-nine prisoners	.	149	"	19	"
" Ciego de Avila.	Five prisoners	.	4	"	"	"
17 Quijada.	Fifty-five prisoners	.	55	"	2 July.	
21 Las Yeguas.	Seven prisoners	.	7	"	25	"
28 Pinalito.	Twenty-nine prisoners	.	29	"	2	"
27 Cuba.	Sixty-six prisoners	.	66	"	27 June.	
30 Cupeyal.	Two prisoners	.	2	"	17 July.	
" La Ciénaga.	Two prisoners	.	2	"	"	"

3237

			3237		
July.					
1 Magayales.	Fifty-four prisoners	.	54	D.	5 July.
2 Jimaguayú.	Two prisoners	.	10	"	10 "
9 Caliba.	One prisoner	.	1	"	1 Ang.
13 Camagüey.	Ninety-two prisoners	.	92	"	1 "
15 Cuba.	Ninety-four prisoners	.	94	"	17 July.
18 Deseada.	Six prisoners	.	6	"	1 Aug.
" Cristal.	Two prisoners	.	3	"	" "
21 Diff places.	Forty prisoners	.	40	"	" "
" Holguin.	Thirty-five prisoners	.	35	"	24 July.
24 Diff. places.	Twelve prisoners	.	12	"	16 Aug.
29 Bueyesito.	Two prisoners	.	2	"	" "
30 Holguin.	One hundred and forty-eight prisoners	.	148	"	30 July.
August.					
5 Doncella.	Capt. Rodolfo Medero and two more	.	3	D.	16 Aug.
11 Guáimaro.	Five prisoners	.	5	"	28 "
12 Rio Grande.	One prisoner	.	1	"	30 "
30 Diff. places.	Twenty prisoners	.	20	"	7 Sept.
September.					
16 Ramon.	José Snarez	.	1	D.	28 Sept.
" Filipinas.	One prisoner	.	1	"	29 "
16 Sopimpa.	One prisoner	.	1	"	29 "
25 Santi Espíritu.	N. Diaz and three more	.	4	"	5 Oct.
27 Matojo.	One prisoner	.	1	"	16 "
October.					
1 Gibaro.	Luis Ramirez Palmarejo	.	1	D.	8 "
" Remedios	Three prisoners	.	3	"	16 "
" Rio Abajo.	Two prisoners	.	2	"	15 "
" Barrabás.	Bernabé Martinez	.	1	"	16 "
" Taguayabon.	Miguel Rivadeneyra	.	1	"	19 "
3 Barrabás.	Pedro Alfonso é Hijo	.	2	"	16 "
3 Manzanillo.	One prisoner	.	1	"	22 "
10 Guisa.	Fifty prisoners	.	50	"	15 "
" Santa Clara.	Two prisoners	.	2	"	16 "
13 Dulce Nombre.	One prisoner	.	1	"	31 "
14 Mate.	Three prisoners	.	3	"	31 "
18 Solis.	Two prisoners	.	2	"	31 "
24 Tunas.	Manuel Alvera and two more	.	3	"	31 "
24 Diff. places.	Six prisoners	.	6	"	2 Nov.
26 Jacinto.	Two prisoners	.	2	"	2 "
26 Diff. places.	Six prisoners	.	6	"	31 Oct.
29 Rensoli.	One prisoner	.	1	"	16 Nov.
f9 Pelayo	One prisoner	.	1	"	16 "
30 Viamonos.	One prisoner	.	1	"	2 "

3860

November.

			3860			
2 Guayo.	Three prisoners	.	3	D.	16	"
3 Diff. places.	Silverio Guerra, S. Mendoza, and three more	.	5	"	"	"
4 Calilla.	One prisoner	.	1	"	11	Dec.
4 Diff. places.	Thirty-seven prisoners	.	37	"	31	"
7 Diff. places.	Three prisoners	.	3	"	16	Nov.
8 Vista Hermosa.	Three prisoners	.	3	"	16	"
8 Sn. Geronimo.	One prisoner	.	1	"	16	"
12 Colorados.	One prisoner	.	1	"	1	Dec.
12 Fajá.	One prisoner	.	1	"	22	Nov.
13 Niguas.	Two prisoners	.	2	"	30	"
14 Canibal.	One prisoner	.	1	"	10	Dec.
" Caigulas	One prisoner	.	1	"	30	Nov.
15 Guasimillo.	Four prisoners	.	1	"	"	"
" Yareyos.	Two prisoners	.	2	"	1	Dec.

December.

11 Ojo de Agua.	Three prisoners	.	3	D.	4	Jan.
" Tunas.	Gerardo P. Puelles and twelve more	.	13	"	4	"
" Manigua Grande.	One prisoner	.	1	"	16	"
23 Camaguey.	C Teodoro Benitez, J A Gironte, and three more	.	5	"	"	"

1873.

January.

3 Buey. Sabana.	One prisoner	.	1	D.	16	Jan.
4 Bella Mata.	Four prisoners	.	4	"	"	"
5 Corojo.	Four prisoners	.	4	"	"	"
5 Remedios.	Three prisoners	.	3	"	"	"
13 Holguin.	Manuel Ruiz	.	1	"	"	"
10 Diff. places.	Eighteen prisoners	.	18	"	"	"
13 Diff. places.	Five prisoners	.	5	"	31	"
24 Jobosi.	One prisoner	.	1	"	"	"
24 Campana.	One prisoner	.	1	"	"	"
26 Diff. places.	Seven prisoners	.	7	"	"	"
28 Diff. places.	Thirteen prisoners	.	13	"	"	"
28 Magibacoa.	One prisoner	.	1	"	"	"
30 Camajuani.	One prisoner	.	1	"	"	"
30 Vigia.	One prisoner	.	1	"	"	"

February.

10 Diff. places.	Eighteen prisoners	,	18	"	16	"
24 Cuba.	One prisoner	.	1	"	2	Mch,
30 Diff. places,	Forty-eight	,	30	"	2	"

4054

March.

			4054			
1	Lauretano.	Two prisoners	2	D.	19 Mar.	
2	Vista Hermosa.	One prisoner	1	"	15	"
3	Najasa.	Eighteen prisoners	18	"	"	"
3	Cauto.	One prisoner	1	"	19	"
6	Sierra.	Cayetano Rustan	1	"	"	"
6	Mijagueto.	N. Maceo	1	"	"	"
6	Calla.	Ten prisoners	10	"	15	"
6	Holguin.	One prisoner	1	"	19	"
10	Diff. places.	Ten prisoners	10	"	19	"
"	Laguna Negra.	One prisoner	1	"	30	"
"	Palmarito.	Nine prisoners	9	"	"	"
"	Yaguas.	P N Valdés and a negro man	2	"	"	"
13	San Martin.	One prisoner	1	"	19	"
15	Diff. places.	Twenty prisoners	20	"	1 Apr.	
23	Najasa.	B Mauri and four more	5	"	26 Mch.	
25	Arteaga.	Eighteen prisoners	18	"	8 Apr.	
28	Holguin.	Five prisoners	5	"	12	"

April.

2	Diff. places.	José Carmenell and eight more	9	D.	16 Apr.	
5	Guaimaro.	Salustiano Girones	1	"	"	"
6	Bueyecito.	One prisoner	1	"	"	"
7	Monte Oscuro.	Five prisoners	5	"	"	"
10	Chorillo.	Nineteen prisoners	19	"	1 May	
12	Joturo.	Twelve prisoners	12	"	"	"
13	Guáimaro.	Five prisoners	5	"	"	"
15	Jarahueca.	Six prisoners	6	"	"	"
"	Cobre.	Six prisoners	6	"	"	"
20	Diff. places.	Twelve prisoners	12	"	"	"
24	Arrieros.	Four prisoners	4	"	3 May.	
24	Hacha.	F Garcia and another	2	"	"	"
24	Jibaro.	Manuel Mendoza	1	"	"	"
29	Camaguey.	Four prisoners	4	"	9 May.	
30	Cantillo.	Two prisoners	2	"	16	"

May.

6	Holguin.	Three prisoners	3	"	9	"
8	Jobos.	One prisoner	1	"	21	"
13	Songo.	One prisoner	1	"	16	"
"	Caobas.	Seventeen prisoners	17	"	16	"
16	Camagüey.	Two prisoners	2	"	18	"
"	Lajas.	One prisoner	2	"	18	"

June.

3	Diff. places.	Sixteen prisoners	16	D.	17 June.	
5	Loreto.	Felix Aguirre	1	"	"	"
8	Guaimaro.	Sixteen prisoners	16	"	"	"

4308

			4308			
9 Jarcial.	One prisoner	.	1	"	"	"
10 Toro.	Three prisoners	.	3	"	"	"
11 Jumento.	One prisoner	.	1	"	"	"
" Gloria.	One prisoner	.	1	"	"	"
19 Caimito.	Three prisoners	.	3	"	29	"
22 Diff. places.	Two prisoners	.	2	"	24	"
30 Pozos.	J R	.	1	"	27 July.	
30 Sau Andrés.	Ten prisoners	.	10	"	"	"

July.

3 Holguin.	Eight prisoners	.	8	D.	9 July	
6 Tacamara.	Three prisoners	.	3	"	10	"
7 Arrierros.	Two prisoners	.	2	"	9	"
7 Tana.	One prisoner	.	1	"	9	"
8 Camaguey.	Seven prisoners	.	7	"	18	"
9 Diego.	M Montero	.	1	"	13	"
10 Júcaro.	Eight prisoners	.	8	"	24	"
12 Zarzal.	E Castillo and J Manso	.	2	"	24	"
14 Matehualo.	Three prisoners	.	3	"	24	"
20 Juau Criollo.	Five prisoners	.	5	"	27	"

August.

4 Castellon.	One prisoner	.	1	D.	12 Aug.	
5 San Cárlos.	Two prisoners	.	2	"	9	"
5 Guaimarillo.	Jesus Riera	.	1	"	15	"
6 Diff. places.	Two prisoners	.	2	"	12	"
8 Jumento.	Three prisoners	.	3	"	15	"
13 Mano Pilon.	One prisoner	.	1	"	20	"
23 Camajuani.	One prisoner	.	1	"	12 Sept.	
" Tunas.	One prisoner	.	1	"	3	"
25 Cobre.	Three prisoners	.	3	"	"	"
" Hondon.	Three prisoners	.	3	"	5	"
" Avispero.	One prisoner	.	1	"	"	"

September.

3 Diff. places.	Three prisoners	.	3	D.	9 Sept.	
8 Cayo Villalvo.	Two prisoners	.	2	"	14	"
8 Palmarito.	Two prisoners	.	2	"	30	"
10 Camajuani.	One prisoner	.	1	"	2 Oct.	
13 Tiarriba.	Two prisoners	.	2	"	28 Sept.	
14 Mabuya.	Juan Gutiso	.	1	"	30	"
" Jobosi.	David Madrigal	.	1	"	"	"
" San Alejandro.	Twenty-seven prisoners	.	27	"	"	"
17 Diff. places.	Two prisoners	.	2	"	2 Oct.	
18 Diff. places.	Thirteen prisoners	.	13	"	20 Sept	
" Santiago.	One prisoners	.	1	"	23	"
" Arrogy Colorado.	One prisoner	.	1	"	30	"

4445

			4445			
20 Tunas.	Five prisoners	.	5	"	28	"
" Diff. places.	Six prisoners	.	6	"	30	"
24 Varas.	One prisoner	.	1	"	30	"
27 Filipina.	One prisoner	.	1	"	"	"

October.

5 Santa Clara.	Captain José	.	1	D.	11	Nov
10 San Diego.	Nine prisoners	.	9	"	1	"
16 Caney.	Three prisoners	.	3	"	11	"
19 Diff. places.	Six prisoners	.	6	"	5	"
23 Diff. places.	Three prisoners	.	3	"	11	"
26 Holguin.	Some prisoners	.	5	"	5	"
28 Jobosi.	One prisoner	.	1	"	11	"
29 Limones.	Two prisoners	.	2	"	1	"
31	One hundred and sixty-three of the Virginians	.	163	"	7	"

November.

1 Guamo.	Five prisoners	.	5	D.	14	Nov
5 Santa Clara.	One Captain	.	1	"	11	"
5 Seborucal.	One prisoner	.	1	"	"	"
7 Sacra.	Ten prisoners	.	10	"	14	"
7 Cubitas.	Three prisoners	.	3	"	15	"
7 San Manuel.	One prisoner	.	1	"	"	"

	4672

CONDEMNED TO DEATH IN GARROTE VIL.

Antonio Fernandez Bramosio, Jacinto Valdés, Nicolas Nin y Pons, Pedro Martin Rivero, Francisco Javier Cisneros, Ambrosio Valiente. Cárlos Manuel de Céspedes, Francisco Vicente Aguilera, Cristóbal Mendoza, Eligio Izaguirre, Eduardo Agramonte, Pedro Maria Agüero y Gonzalez, Salvado Cisneros Betancourt, Francisco Sanchez Betancourt, Pio Rosado, Fernando Fornaris, Miguel Betancourt Guerra, Jesus Rodriguez, José Izagnirre, Miguel Gerónimo Gutierrez, Arcadio Garcia, Tranquilino Valdes, Antonio Lorda, Eduardo Machado, Antonio Zambrana, Ignacio Agramonte, Rafael Morales, Lucas del Castillo, Diego Machado, Ramon Perez Trujillo, Manuel Quesada, Thomas Jordan, Francisco Ruz, José Valiente, José Maria Mora, Antonio Fernandez Bramosio, José Francisco Bassora, Francisco Izquierdo, Plutarco Gonzalez, Ramon Fernandez Criado, Francisco Javier Cisneros, Joaquin Delgado, Ramon Aguirre, Francisco Fesser, Ignacio Alfaro, Miguel Aldama, Carlos del Castillo, José Manuel Mestre, Hilario Cisneros, Leonardo Delmonte, José Maria Céspedes, Francisco Valdes Mendoza, Nestor Ponce de Leon, Federico Galvez, Francisco Javier Balmaseda, Manuel Casanova, Antonio Mora, Luis Felipe Mantilla, Manuel Marquez, José Peña and Joaquin Anido.

6   March   10

55

			1871
Santiago—One hundred persons.	100	D.	11 Mch.
José Godino.	1	"	13 July.
Sagua—Santiago Feo.	1	"	23 "
Pablo Feo.	1	"	" "
Nené Feo.	1	"	" "
Pto Príncipe—Enrique Flotás and Carlos Rivero.	2	"	29 Aug.
Sta Clara—Francisco Cárdenas Perez.	1	"	5 Sept.
Baldomero Cancia y Garcia.	1	"	" "
Pto Príncipe—Ignacio Gonzalez y Gonzalez.	1	"	" "
Antonio Rodriguez Gonzalez.	1	"	" "
Bayama—Arcadio Remon.	1	"	3 Nov.
Juan Francisco Aguirre, Martin Aguirre, Manuel Lopez Piñeiro, Félix Fuentes, P. M. Rivero, J. M. Mayorga, Hilario Cisneros, R. I. Arnao, J. M. Céspedes, J. B de Luna, F V Mendoza, Federico Galvez, Rafael M. Merchan, Tomás Rodriguez, Miguel Leiva Salmon, Joaquin Jaramillo, Cristobal Diaz, Pedro Bernal.	19		Official Gazette, July, 1873.

191

COURT MARTIALED BY ORDER OF THE CAPTAIN GENERAL AS PUNISHABLE UNDER THE DECREE OF FEBRUARY THE 12TH, 1869.

Silverio Padilla, Tranquiino Garcia Machado, Rafael Lubian, Julian Mendive, Tirso Silvestre.	5	D.	27 July.
José Capiro, Francisco Martinez Pupo, Eligio Machado, Eugenio Herrero, José D. Gonzalez, Manuel Alvarez.	6	"	29 "
Francisco Casamadrid.	1	"	2° Aug.
Benjamin Perez Figneroa, Cesareo Betancourt, Antonio Ramirez.	3	"	5 "
José Antonio Aguilera, Angel Cedeño, Jesus Curbelo, Fernando Suarez, Antonio Garces, Narciso Cardel, José Ramon Rodriguez.	7	"	7 "
Gregorio Ramirez, Antonio Cancio Bello, Isidro del Pino Perez, Manuel Leon Bonilla, Antonio Javier Martinez, Victorio Arbelo, Emilio Puente Avila.	7	"	19 "
Francisco Diaz, José Diaz, Rafael Oropesa, Guillermo Miró, Manuel Perez, Casimiro Chongo, Dr. Ramon Barrios, Manuel Lantigua Rodriguez, Amelio Luis Vila de los Reyes, José Diaz Piñeira, Juan Alvarez Campa.	11	"	21 "
Miguel Capriles, Joaquin Gonzalez, Mariano Gonzalez, Domingo Reinoso, Francisco Antonio Zayas	5	"	25 "
Esteban Lima.	1	"	28 "
Julian Argüelles, Antonio Maria Perez.	2	"	29 "
José Garcigorta y Galan, Manuel del Sol.	2	"	2 Sept
José E. Colima.	1	"	5 "
GERTRUDIS NAPOLES.	1	"	16 "
Pro. Pedro Yera, VICTORIA VALDES, CARMEN CORREA, ROSARIO CORTAZAR, PLACIDA, ROSA Y DOLORES PEREZ, Pedro Correa, Pedro Carbonell, Juan Urdaneta, Bamon Cortazar, Mateo, Antonio, Rafael y José Eulogio Alfonso y Blas Perez.	15	"	23 "
Ramon Perez, Emilio Manrique, Francisco Echeropal, Eduardo Zamora.	4	"	26 "
Carlos Alvarez, Antonio Amado, Salomé Sandoval.	3	"	3 Oct.
Zacarias Lopez.	1	"	6 "
Justo y Ascencio Gonzalez, Matias Macias.	3	"	12 "
José Luis Aguilera.	1	"	23 Dec.
Liborio Jiminez	1	"	2 Jan.
Manuel del Aguila.	1	"	6 "
Juan B. Latta, Camilo Hernandez, Juan B Colonia.	3	"	11 "

84

CONDEMNED TO HARD LABOR FOR LIFE IN THE CHAIN
GANG OF THE PENAL COLONY OF CEUTA.

1869.

Rafael Lanza, Isidro Hernandez, José A. Lucena,
Julian Sanchez Villavicencio.   4   Sept. 14
Pedro Rivera.   1   Dec.   30

CONDEMNED TO TEN YEARS HARD LABOR IN THE CHAIN
GANG OF THE PENAL COLONY OF CEUTA.

1869.

Miguel Estrada Mirandi, Ramon J. Agramonte, José
Felix Bonachea, Josa Ruiz Lopez, Leonardo Perez y
Martinez.   5   Sept. 14

CONDEMNED TO EIGHT YEARS HARD LABOR IN THE CHAIN
GANG OF THE PENAL COLONY OF CEUTA.

1869.

José Valera, Tomas Gener, Anibal Agüero, José Roque
Sanchez, José Manuel Pascual, Alberto Agüero,
Cárlos Callejas, José Eligio Perez, Gregorio Gon-
zalez, Ricardo Horta, Juan B. Juanicot, Antonio
Guichard, Joaquin Melville, Miguel Vidal, Ignacio
Martinez, Liborio Delgado, Andres Arongo, Angel
Valladares, José Guiteras, José Zamora.   20   May   26

CONDEMNED TO SIX YEARS HARD LABOR IN THE CHAIN
GANG OF THE PENAL COLONY OF CEUTA

1869.

Antonio Alva Moreno.   1   Sept   14

CONDEMNED TO TEN YEARS HARD LABOR IN THE CHAIN
GANG.

1869.

Manuel de Jesus Fleites, Tomas Manuel Juviel,
Miguel Fernandez, Manuel Capote Quiñones.   4   Sept. 14
Cayetano N.   1 · Nov.   2

CONDEMNED TO EIGHT YEARS HARD LABOR IN THE CHAIN
GANG.

1869.

Casimiro Gonzalez, Antonio Abad.   2   Sept. 14

CONDEMNED TO SIX YEARS HARD LABOR IN THE CHAIN
GANG.

1869.

Antonio José and Tiburcio de la Cruz, Juan Sanchez,
Jesus M. Meneses, Demetrio Peña.   6   Aug.   6
Meliton Valdes, Fidel Barrera (hijo)   2   Sept.   14
Pedro Ulet Delgado, Manuel Lopez Sierra, Julian
Mendive.   8   Nov.   2
José Lorenzo Castañeda.   1   Nov.   2

CONDEMNED TO FOUR YEARS HARD LABOR IN THE CHAIN
CHAIN GANG.

1869.

José Camilo Enriquez.   1   Aug.   6
Julian José Acosta, Eduardo Merlo.   2   Nov.   2

CONDEMNED FROM TWO TO TEN YEARS HARD LABOR IN THE
GANG.

1869.

Enrique Rodriguez, Vicente Paleu.   2   Sept.   14
Agustin Morell, Alonso de Céspedes, Nieves Cardoso
and Nicolas Sardinas.   4   Nov.   2
             N. Emilio.   D.   13 July.
             Two of the Hornet.   2   "   29 Jan.
Jan. 12   N Arias.   1   "   14 "
March 1
Cienfuegos—Matias Suarez.   1   "   3 Mch.
July 12
Santiago—Rafael Palacio, Franco Caballero, Miguel
             Echeverria, Tomás Ferrer.   4   "   20 July.
Villa Clara—Rafael Alfonso, Domingo Sosa Ramiez,
             Desiderio Ordoñez, Manuel.   4   D.   5 Sept.
Santiago—Juan José Torres: 1   D.   13 July.
Güines—Juan Rodriguez Valmaseda.   1   "   2 Nov.
Sagua—José Cantero.
             Manuel Herrera Gallardo.   2   "   23 July.
Manzanillo—Juan Rafael Cisneros.   1   "   21 Nov.
Villa Clara—Nazario Rodriguez Fco.
             Martin Bello y Ruiz.   2   "   12 Dec.
             Miguel Machado.   1   "   25 Nov.
Camaguezy—José Casto del Valle and 3 negroes.   4   "   14 Dec.
Santiago—Juan de Dios Dupuy.   1   "   17 "
Pto Principe—Juan de Dios Acosta.   1   "   "   "
Remedios—Manuel Quintanal.
             Benigno del Rio.   2   "   8 Dec.

Santa Clara—Rafael Vila Chaves.		
Pedro del Rio.	2 "	8 Dec.
Manzanillo—Dionisio Gutierrez.	1 "	21 Nov.
Habana—Eleven students.	11 "	28 "
Joaquin Bermudez, Joaquin Rodriguez.	2 "	13 July.
Habana—Nineteen students.	19 "	28 Nov.
Pto Principe—Polonio Cisneros.	1 "	23 May.
José M. y Cabrera.	2 "	28 Dec.
Manzanillo—Miguel Rodriguez Navea.	1 "	21 Nov.
Remedios —José A. Espinosa.	1 "	8 Dec.
Santa Clara—Pedro Herrera.	1 "	" "
santiago—Jesus M M.	1 "	23 July.
Santiago—Juana Perez.	1 "	5 Sept.
Habana—Four students.	4 "	28 Nov.
Six of the Hornet.	6 "	29 Jan.
Nov. 2.		
Habana—Sixty-six men and a woman.	67 "	3 Nov.
Pto Principe—Lino Cabrera.	1 "	28 Dec.
Pto Principe—Jorge Ayala, Gervasio Varona, Venancio Lopez Pacho, Anto. Lopez Cañas.	4 "	23 May.

TRANSPORTED TO THE ISLAND OF FERNANDO POO IN THE COAST OF
AFRICA ON THE 21ST MAY, 1869.

Acosta, D. Alejandro.
Acosta y Romero, D. Alejandro.
*Acosta, D. Domingo.
*Almanza, D. Blas José.
Almanza, D. Cárlos Enrique.
Agüero, D. Martin.
Agüero, D. Federico.
Armengol, D. Francisco W.
Ayala, D. Felipe Cárlos de
*Albernas, D. José Leon.
Anduiza, D. Juan.
*Arce, D. Miguel.
*Armario, D. Ramiro.
Andino, D. Vicente.
Alvares, D. Nicolás.
Abreu, D. Manuel.
Alvarez, D. Mannel.
André D. Domingo.
Boggiero, D. Andrés.
Boloña, D. Antonio.
Baliño D. Cárlos José
Broderman, D. Julio.
Bianchi, D. Joaquin
Barrenqui, D. Pedro Luis.
Bravo Senties, D. Miguel.
Barreto, D. Antonio.
Barreto, D. Indalecio.
Barreto, D. Manuel.
Bonachea, D. Alejo.
*Bonachea, D. Francisco C.
Balmaseda, D. Francisco Javier.
Balmaseda, D. Enrique.
Balmaseda, D. Crispin.
Balmaseda, D. Antonio Abad.
*Balmaseda, (pardo) Simon.
*Blanco, D. Juan Bautista.
Blanco, D. Julian.
Blanco, D. Luis.
Benitez, D. Juan Bautista.
Bellido de Luna, D. Antonio.
Calvo, D. Félix Maria
Castillo, Pro. D. Alfo del
Castillo, D. Cárlos del
Castillo, (mor. esc.) J. María

Cabaleiro, D. José.
Cabaleiro, D. Eduardo.
*Caballero D. Emilio.
Cairo, D. Francisco.
*Calero, D. Gabriel.
Cabañas, D. José.
Cárdenas, D. Juan.
Castañeda, D. José.
Cordobes, D. Manuel.
Cantero, D. Miguel G.
Casals y Quesada, D. Pedro.
Cauto, D. Miguel.
Canto, D. Miguel Liborio.
Ceballos, D. Antonio.
Chirino, D. Pablo.
Chenard, D. José Maria.
Chaves, D. Ambrosio.
Cherse, D. Antolin.
Deleito, D. Rafael.
Du-Breuil, D. Alfredo.
Duran, D. Francisco.
Duggan, D. Juan.
Diaz, D. Ricardo.
Diaz Pimienta, D. Diego.
*Diaz Regalado, D. Santiago.
*Diaz, D. Pedro.
Diaz, D. Andrés.
*Echemendia, D. Francisco.
Echemendía D. Hermógenos.
Echagarrua, D. Benito.
*Esverel, D. Pedro.
Espinache, D. Eduardo.
Embil, D. Miguel.
*Espinosa, D. Simon.
Feo, D. Antonio.
Fuentes, D. Félix.
Freixas, D. Patrocinio.
Fors, D. Cárlos.
Fors, D. Rafael.
Farres, D. Santiago.
Farres, D. Francisco.
Farres, D. Enrique.
*Fradera, D. Andrés.
Fernandez, D. Eugenio.

Fernandez de Velasco, D. Frco.
Fernandez Morera, D. José M.
Gonzalez, D. Andrés Avelino.
*Gonzalez, D. José Antonio.
Gonzalez, D. José Bienvenido.
Gonzalez Alvarez, D. Juan.
*Gonzalez, D. Paulino.
Gonzalez, D. Ricardo.
*Gonzalez, D. Ramon.
Gonzalez, D. Felipe.
Garrido, D. Cayetano Domingo.
García D. Federico.
Garcia, D. José Maria.
García Cáceres, D. Joaquin.
García, D. José del Cármen.
García, D. Luis.
*García, D. Nicolás Donato.
Galvan D. José
Gutierrez, D. Jesus María
*Galiano, D. Manuel.
*Hedesa, D. Antonio.
Huguet, D. José.
Hoyos Presbítero, D. J. Miguel
*Izaqui, D. Antonio
*Infanzon, D. Maduel María.
Lima, D. Jacinto.
Lima, D. Miguel.
Lamar, D. Evaristo.
Mazon, D. Andres.
Montes, D. Cayetano.
Mujica, D. Manuel Antonio.
Mujica, (pardo esclavo) Cárlos.
Marquez, D. Francisco.
Meneiga, D. Francisco.
Milan, D. Gaspar.
Macías, D. José Miguel.
Monzon, D. José
Mora, D. José Manuel.
Momplet, D. José.
Marrero, D. Antonio.
Marrero y Enrique, D. Bartolomé
Marrero, D. Francisco.
Marrero, D. Tiburcio.
Martin, D. Cárlos.
*Medero, D. Bonifacio.
*Medero, D. Tomás.
Morales, D. Cárlos.
Morales, (pardo) J. Evangelista.

Molina, D. Eduvigis.
*Meza, D. José.
Moya, D. José Antonio.
Moya, D. Pedro.
Martinez Suri, D. Marcelino.
Martinez, D. Manuel.
Mendive, D. Mariano.
Navarro, D. Antonio.
*Nuñez, D. José.
*Norel, D. Joaquin.
*Ovando, D. Federico.
*O'Connell, D. Cárlos.
Ortega, D. Cárlos.
*Ortega, D. José de la Luz.
Oller, D. Fernando.
Olivero, D. José Ignacio.
Ortiz, D. José Inés.
Oliva, D. Pedro.
Pozo, D. José Julian.
Parodi, D. Estéban.
Pantaleon, D. Estéban.
Parilla, D. Justo.
Palacios, D. Luis.
Posada, D. Bamon.
Pulgaron, D. Rafael.
*Padrino, D. Rafael.
Perez, D. Antonio.
Perez, Torres, D. Andrés.
Perez, D. Benjamin.
Perez, D. Felipe.
Perez, de Pablo.
*Perez de la Hera, D. Silvestre.
*Perez, D. Salvador.
*Perez Angueira, D. Francisco.
Perez, D. Severino.
Perez, D. Francisco.
Penichet, D. Ramon.
Poey, D. Federico.
Ponce de Leon, D. José Manuel.
Peña, D. Bartolomé.
Peña, D. José, Antonio de la
Peña, D. Mariano de la
Pereira, D. José.
Pino, (hijo) D. Rafael.
Pino (padre) D. Rafael.
Quinteroy Angueira, de Eduardo.
Quintana, D, José Maria.
Quintana, D. Pedro.

Morales Mena, Rafael.
Morales Julien, D. Rafael.
Rubí, D. Martin.
*Reinaldo, Jacobó Gregori.
Rosell, D. José.
*Ricaño, D. José María.
Raldiris, D. Lino.
Rojas, D. Manuel J.
Riquelme, D. Miguel.
Rubio, D. Ramon.
Rio, D. Andres del
Rio, D. Joaquin del
Riveron, D. Augustin.
Riveron, D. José.
Riveron, D. Pedro.
Roselló D. Cayetano.
*Riera, D. Francisco.
Ramos, D. Juan Tomás.
Ramos Almeida, D. Francisco.
Rodriguez, D. José María.
Rodriguez, D. Lucas.
Rodriguez D. Leandro.
*Rodriguez, D. Manuel.
Rodriguez D. Mariano.
Reus, D. Ramon.
Sebe D. Andres.
Salouvel, D. Juan.
*Sandoval D. Angel.
Saez. D. Dionisio.
*Segura, D. Eusebio.
Sotol ngo, D. Fracisco de
Sanchez Lubian, D. Francisco.
Sanchez, D. José.

Rozas, Mr. John C.
*Riva, D. Diego José.
Socarras, D. Indalecio.
Socarras, D. Juan Francisco.
Socarras, D. Pablo.
Sosa, D. Juan.
Sta. Cruz, Pro. D. José Cecilio.
Salinas D. Manuel.
*Salaverria, de Pedro.
Salazar, D. Rafael.
Sal y Lima, Pro. D. Rafael.
Someillan, D. Pedro C.
Torre, D. Juan de la
Trujillo y Carrera, D. José.
Trujillo y Armas, D. Manuel.
Tarafa, D. Miguel.
Urrutia, D. José.
*Valerio. D. Felipe.
Walls y Wilson, D. José.
Walls y Wilson, D. Santiago.
Vidal, D. Isidro.
Valle, D. Ramon.
*Vargas, D. Ladislao.
Valdes Chacon, D. Ambrosio.
Valdes, Pro. D. José Cándido.
Valdes Colon, D. Joaquin.
Valdes, (pardo) José Miguel.
Valdes (pardo) José.
Zavas, D. Eraclio.
Zifredo. D. Hipólito.
Zifredo, D. Juan.
Zimmermann, D. Cárlos.
*Zerezo, (moreno) Alejandro.

* Died on the ship or in the hospital after landing on account of the bad treatment, exposure. bad aliments and want of medicines,

The professions of the above montioned 250 transported Cubans were :

7 Administrators of sugar plantations.
1 Architect.
3 Attorneys-at-law.
3 Brokers.
2 Bankers.
10 Carpenters.
5 Clergymen.
11 Clerks of Notaries, Lawyers, &c.
4 Druggists.
3 Distillers.
4 Engineers.
20 Farmers.
2 Judges of the peace.
6 Lawyers.
4 Masons.
4 Military officers.
2 Mortgage Recorders.
8 Notaries.

33 Clerks of Merchants.	6 Physicians.
6 " of Railroads.	1 President of a Gas Company.
2 " of the Post Office.	1 Painter of history.
1 Consul of Great Britain.	17 Property holders.
3 Dentists.	7 Teachers.
3 Police Officers.	5 Tobacco Manufacturers.
2 Pilots.	1 Tailor.
5 Sugar Masters.	15 Sailors, musicians, boat-
4 Surveyors.	men, sugar makers, jour-
3 Students.	neymen, and other pro-
3 Shoemakers.	fessions.
1 Schoolboy.	
2 Silversmiths.	250 of whom were

Clergymen. - - - 5.
Married. - - - - 140.
Single. - - - - 91.
Widowers. - - - 14.

250.

TRANSPORTED TO THE PENAL COLONIES OF AFRICA.

Calixto Machado Marin.	1	Aug. 5
Luis Marin de la Cruz,	1	Aug. 6
José de Jesus Quintana, Faustino Cepeda.	2	Aug. 12
Bernardo J. Esverel, Domingo Zaza, José Gabriel Flores, Manuel Sanchez, Enrique Miranda, Ramon Zenea, Felix Clarke, Rafael Gutierrez, José Valdes.	9	Aug. 17
Carlos Valcour, Juan Francisco Miranda Manuel Suarez del Pino, Pablo Fuente, Laureano Carrasco Juan Bejarano.	6	Aug. 19
Tomas Toledo, Juan M. Rey, Valentin Gomez.	3	Aug. 21
Carlos Diaz Molina, Andres de la Torre, Antonio Fluriack y Sariol.	3	Sept. 5
Felipe and and Andres Rivera, Juan Hernandez, Ramon Rodriguez, Gregorio Perez, Francisco Alvarez, José Antonio Rivera.	7	Sept. 12
Francisco Blandino.	1	Sept. 16
Miguel and José Valdes.	2	Sept. 18
Miguel and José Almeida, José M. Oliver, Miguel Oquendo.	4	Sept. 23
Carlos Armijio y Martinez.	1	Oct. 8
Petronilo de Velasco.	1	Oct. 15
Pedro Luis Perchemiel.	1	Oot. 30
Antonio Ramos Almeida.	1	Dic. 14
Federico Mariño.	1	Dic. 18

www.ingramcontent.com/pod-product-compliance
Lightning Source LLC
Chambersburg PA
CBHW030020030726
47499CB00008B/3057